RISE

Populations Crumble, Book 2

K. A. Gandy

THIGPEN-GANDY PUBLISHING

For Dustin, who has grown with me, changed with me, and loved me through all of our ups and downs. When we succeed, we do it together.
Always my love.

CONTENTS

ONE

BUYER'S REMORSE

"What do you mean, your name isn't Patrick O'Roarke? I just married you, and *now* you want to tell me your name isn't your name?" I say, my voice tight with incredulity, hurt, and fury.

"It's not as bad as it sounds, I promise!" He raises both hands in a calming gesture, but I'm having none of it.

"I have had it up to here with this nonsense of keeping me in the dark! What is your name, if it's not Patrick O'Roarke? Are we even legally married? Who the heck are you?" I demand, fury winning the emotional battle for the moment.

"I'm Patrick, yes. But my last name isn't O'Roarke. It's Royce. Patrick Royce. The marriage license has my correct legal name." He gestures cautiously toward the desk, as if I might bite him.

"Care to tell me why you felt the need to hide your real name from me? From everyone, for that matter? It's O'Roarke in the Bachelor Book, so I don't know how you pulled that off." I stand up and start pacing the length of the director's office in agitation. I can't even look at him. Oh, crap on a cracker—I married this man not two hours ago and I already caught him in a lie.

What else has been a lie? What if he lied about his feelings for me, too? Hurt surges to the forefront, but I try not to show it.

Keep it together, Sadie. You have to find out what's going on.

"It wasn't just you, it was everyone. Even Glitch doesn't know my real name. The director didn't either until today, when I had to have my legal name put on the marriage license, or else the marriage wouldn't have been valid. And I didn't want that; I want to be married to you!" His voice goes up slightly at the end, and it's clear he's trying very hard to convince me. *It's not working, you lying S-O-B.*

"Is that supposed to make it all better? To know that you lied to everyone, and not only me? You still haven't answered me. Why are you lying to us all?" I snap, not giving him an inch—despite my heart fracturing in my chest.

"Does the name Royce really not ring any bells? You don't recognize it at all? You're a smart girl, Sadie. I wouldn't lie to you if I had an option. This all moved so fast, I didn't know how to spring it on you when you went from five matches to 'I do' in a matter of days! I couldn't risk telling you until it was certain, and then it went from certain to here so quickly I didn't know when was the right time to break the news." Now he's standing too, and he rakes his hand through his hair in frustration.

"Tell. Me. Why." I stop pacing, and face him head on. Chin up, arms folded. "Tell me the truth, right freaking now, or I'm going to walk out of here and tell everyone what a two-faced liar you are!" My voice has gone cold, and I don't care. There's *nothing* I hate worse than a liar. *How are we supposed to build a real marriage if I can't trust him?* The thought makes me want to curl up in a ball and cry, but that's not an option right now.

He lets out a frustrated groan. "My father is the prime minister!" he half shouts.

I'm dumbstruck by the revelation. That is not what I was expecting him to say. Not that I know what I expected, but still. "Prime minister? As in, prime minister of the entire NAA? Prime minister that's been in office for so long, they want to name him as *monarch* of the North American Alliance? That's your father?"

"Yes, *that* prime minister. He was voted in when I was ten, and he's been unanimously re-elected every year since. The name Royce is recognized across the entire NAA, and I had no chance of ever being known on my own merit as long as I was using it. So, I asked his security team to make me an identity packet with a different name. O'Roarke is my mom's family name. I just wanted to be judged for myself, not who my father is. Please, Sadie. Please tell me you can understand that, and forgive me for not telling you sooner?"

My mind is reeling. He told me he spent so much time with his friend growing up because his parents traveled for his dad's job. He told me that his father was always working, and his parents were rarely there for holidays to visit due to his demanding job. Somehow he managed to never mention *what* that job was exactly, even though he had ample opportunities.

My anxious pacing resumes, as my mind grapples with the implications of the fact that I've just married this man who has a very political family. Part of the reason I'd chosen him over the six other options was because I thought he was a normal guy. Someone who could appreciate my family and my home, without being endlessly pulled away. *It wasn't the only reason, though. I've fallen for him, hook, line, and sinker.* Those hopes are dashed upon the rocks of reality, and the sun hasn't risen on the second day of our marriage yet. *How could I not know he was lying to me?*

"Oh, God. If the lawmakers succeed in changing our government to a monarchy, everyone says your father would be made king." I grab the end of my veil and worry the bottom hem nervously. "That would make you a prince, right? Next in line to rule the entire freaking continent? Oh, God, Patrick! I'm *not* cut out to be a queen, you know that, right? Surely you knew that when you let me choose you. Why would you do that?" I meet his gaze anxiously, only to find him infuriatingly silent. "Would you say something? You can't drop this all on me and let me drown in it!"

"I'm sorry, it seemed like you needed a minute to process. The monarchy situation has come up many times over the years and been shot down each time. There are plenty of people who have encouraged me to follow in my father's footsteps, but I have no political inclinations. I wouldn't have gotten a new name and hired on to be an NLC guard if I wanted to go into politics." His expression is intense, and regret is plain in the way he's staring at me, eyebrows down and lips pursed.

Well, when you put it like that, it does sound absurd. I let out a shaky breath. Maybe it isn't quite that level of catastrophe. More of a normal, lying-son-of-a-gun level catastrophe. Okay, I can handle that.

"What happens if I refuse to sign?" I force my voice to stay flat, controlled. The roller coaster of emotions in my chest will have to wait until later. "I don't exactly appreciate marrying someone who's lied to me from the moment we met."

His face clouds, but he answers, "I don't know. I'm not sure it makes a difference at this point. We've already had the ceremony, and there are quite a few witnesses that you willingly married me. Refusal to sign the document now probably wouldn't go over well with the director . . . and frankly, we still haven't figured out what they did with Josephine. I don't want to know what they'd do to you."

I feel like I'm picking up on an undercurrent of something in his words, whether pain or anger I can't quite tell. Regardless, he brought this on himself. I trusted him, and he was lying to me. He's not wrong about Josephine, though. She caused a scene in a gathering, and hasn't been seen or heard from since. We'd chosen our honeymoon location primarily to check up on a lead we'd gotten that she'd been moved there. I angrily stalk over to the desk, pick up a pen, and sign my name. The letters are shorter and more jagged than usual, but I don't think anyone cares.

Slapping the pen back to the desk, I level him with an angry look, to cover the pain. "Don't think you're off the hook for this. I understand why you want to be your own person and live a normal life; that doesn't mean I forgive you for choosing to marry me under false pretenses." I pause, looking down at the floor, and notice that the tulle of my gorgeous wedding gown looks less magical in the harsh office lighting than when I put it on a few hours ago, and was still full of hope and butterflies. "I don't believe in divorce, Patrick. I really meant to make it work with you, and I don't know how to feel about you right this minute. But, I also have an obligation to see this through, whether I like it or not. And my brother and Faith are out there on that shuttle, waiting for a pair of happy newlyweds to accompany them on our honeymoon. We *are* going to tell them about this, but I don't think now is the time." The irony of that is not lost on me, but no harm will come to them if I sleep on this news for a night, rather than ruin their wedding night.

He gives me a single, sharp nod. "Are you ready to go? Or do you have more questions?"

To his credit, he has taken my anger well. Not that he shouldn't—it's justified. But that doesn't matter to all men.

"Yes, we shouldn't keep them waiting; it's a long drive to Mairmont."

"Okay then, let's get going." He walks to the door and holds it open for me, still a gentleman. As we walk down the hallway, there is no sign of the director or anyone else other than the sounds of merriment still coming from the dining hall. What I wouldn't give to go back to the blissful ignorance I'd had barely an hour ago, sitting and enjoying my wedding dinner. Turns out the deal I made was with a devil, and unknowingly or not—there's no going back.

Turns out, the shuttle was only to take us to the local airport. Todd the ever-pleasant shuttle driver handed us over to Deon, the pilot, and then turned right around, presumably to await more brides at the NLC.

The four of us were quickly guided aboard by a smiling male flight attendant after the quick meet and greet with Deon. He offered us all drinks before urging us to strap in. The flat screen at the front of the plane informed us that we were on a 1670 super-jet, and our arrival time in Mairmont was estimated to be an hour and a half.

"I've never been on an airplane before," I say to no one in particular, nerves starting to hit.

Faith spins from her position in the row ahead of me, and gives me a reassuring smile. "It's very safe, and so much faster than the shuttle! Takeoff can be a bit unsettling, but after that it is really easy to pretend you're on a super-fast shuttle." She settles back in, and through the seat crack I see her grab Teddy's hand. My stomach clenches, and I glance out the corner of my eye at Patrick, who's just staring straight ahead. His hand is lying there, but I'm far too stubborn to reach out and take it. Instead, I opt to check my seatbelt for the third time, as Deon's voice comes over the sound system.

"All right, newlyweds! We're taking off for Mairmont, and the skies are clear. We should be arriving in roughly ninety minutes. Please remain seated and buckled in until Martin comes around with your refreshments." There is a ding indicating the end of the announcement, and then the plane lurches into motion. Trying not to appear startled, I fix my attention out the window. Our speed picks up rapidly, and the feeling of the earth being sucked away from the bottom of the plane makes my stomach do an angry flip. However, it only lasts a moment before we are airborne.

"Whooo!" Teddy raises his and Faith's clasped hands in the air. "That'll make you feel alive, am I right?" He turns with a huge grin on his face, which I return the best I can. "What's wrong, baby sister—getting queasy? You're not pregnant already, are you?" He gives Patrick a fake scowl before laughing and settling back down.

Definitely not. I mentally grumble.

The flight passes uneventfully except for heavenly cinnamon cookies that Martin brought us once it was safe to be up and about. I may have had thirds, but that's nobody's business. Patrick and I are mostly silent, but Faith and Teddy are too wrapped in their bubble of infatuation to notice.

The landing leaves much to be desired, but I'm thankful we are safely back on solid ground. If only I could say the same about my marriage.

Two

NEW ARRIVALS

The weather is cold but clear when we embark from the plane, and the wind bites through the thin lacy top of my gown. I rub my arms fruitlessly while we wait for a shuttle to pick us up, and then tuck my hands under my armpits. Despite keeping my complaints to myself, I feel a warm jacket settle around my shoulders.

Startled, I look up and see Patrick in just his white button up shirt. He must have ditched the vest during dinner. "Thank you. Aren't you going to get cold?" I ask, already tugging the jacket onto my arms.

"No, I'm pretty warm blooded, I'll be fine. You don't have much coverage in that dress, beautiful though it is," he says, voice reserved. The gap between us is yawning wide open, and my heart tugs painfully that I put it there. *But I didn't, he did when he lied to me.*

"Hey, you save that for later. I know you two are married now but it weirds me out watching somebody romance my baby sister." Teddy has his arms wrapped around Faith's shoulders in a loving embrace, and her head is tucked tightly into his chest to ward off the chill.

She elbows him in the ribs, and he pretends he's mortally wounded. "My knees are freezing! This shuttle needs to hurry it up," she says, voicing all of our discomfort.

As if summoned by her words, it pulls into view and stops in front of us. The doors whoosh open, and down comes a smiling driver. "Hello everyone! My name is Todd, and I'll be your driver today. Is this all of the luggage?"

We all stare blankly at him, but my brain catches up faster than the rest of the group. "Todd, really?"

Now he looks confused. "Yes, is there a problem?"

"No, it's just our driver back in Georada was also Todd. It's a small world, I guess." I explain our puzzled reaction.

"Oh, yeah, I've met that Todd. Good guy. All right, feel free to find a cozy seat, and we'll be on our way shortly." His smile is friendly as he turns to load up our bags.

Shuffling aboard with the giant gowns still weighing us down, we see that this shuttle is fitted with love seats, instead of individual chairs like the NLC shuttles. "Gotta push us together at every opportunity." I mumble to myself.

"What'd you say, sis?" Teddy asks.

"Nothing, just noting the new seating arrangements," I say.

Faith takes the front row, so we settle in behind them. My puffy dress takes up about two thirds of the bench seat, despite my efforts to keep it to my side. I'm making yet another futile attempt to snatch it back to my side of the loveseat when Patrick reaches over and stops my hand gently with his.

"It's fine, Sadie. Leave it," he says gently.

It may be petty, but part of me wants as much space between us as possible. I let it go reluctantly and lean back against the seat. The dress springs over and encompasses Patrick's shins the instant I do. *Traitor.* I mentally chastise the sparkly tulle.

Mairmont Todd climbs back aboard, and in his chipper tone tells us the bathrooms are in the back, and we should arrive in about forty five minutes. He quickly settles into the driver's seat, and then we're on our way.

Faith pops up to visit the ladies' room, and Patrick excuses himself as well. Teddy turns around and levels me with a knowing look.

"What's wrong? You're acting weird," he asks.

"Nothing, just tired." I feel guilty for lying to him, but I don't want to ruin his wedding night. This isn't his problem, it's mine. *I'm the idiot who fell for the liar.* I give him a smile, but I can tell it's weak.

"Uh-huh. Yeah, tired. Are you nervous? Scared? Need the talk? Wait, please don't say you need the talk." He pauses for a second, mulling it over. "Oh, actually it's fine. I'm married now, Faith can give you the talk—she's done this before." He seems pleased with this revelation.

I just shake my head at him. "No, I'm fine. Really, just tired. Also should you be foisting stuff off on your wife already? Isn't it a little early in the game to start bad habits?" I rib, hoping to distract him from my issues.

He scoffs. "Bad habits? Best habits, you mean."

Patrick makes his way back to our seat, and scooches in past my voluminous gown. Faith is back a minute later, and to my utter mortification Teddy does not let the conversation drop.

"Hey, babe, Sadie here has wedding night nerves. Think you can give her a pep talk?" He waggles his eyebrows at her, and she smacks his chest. Patrick stiffens beside me.

"Teddy! Leave your sister alone." She turns to face me. "If you *actually* want to talk, you know I'm always here. We sisters have to be there for each other, right?" The smile she gives me is warm, and I can tell she really means it.

I smile back, appreciating the sentiment. "Thanks Faith, but I think I'm okay."

She settles back into her seat, and Teddy slips his arm back around her. She rests her head on his shoulder, and my heart clenches painfully. I force myself to look out the window instead, as the scenery slips by in the darkness. The drive slips by in silence, and then we're pulling up in front of what appears to be a large guest house. The white board siding reflects in the moonlight, looking old and stately. I can't see much else, but I can hear the ocean close by, and taste the salt in the air as we step off the shuttle stairs.

Pink-shirted staff come out and take our bags from Todd, and an older gentleman with slicked back salt-and-pepper hair approaches us.

"Good evening, newlyweds! My name is Jared, and I'm so pleased to welcome you to the Mairmont Honeymoon Resort! We're so glad you chose to start your new family with us. Please follow me inside, and we'll get you settled into your rooms as quickly as possible." He turns and leads us into the guest house. "Gentlemen, if you'd step over here, I have a few things to discuss with you. Ladies, there are hot beverages and fresh pastries on the side board; do help yourselves. I'll have your dashing grooms back to you momentarily." He may be older, but the toothpaste-ad grin he shoots us could be Eric's twin.

Faith and I go inspect the pastries, and once we've both gotten one, we take a seat in one of the plush wingback chairs surrounding the sitting area. I've got a cheese Danish halfway to my mouth when she asks quietly, "Are you sure you're okay? I was serious earlier, I don't mind talking with you if you've got questions. Or concerns. Anything you need to know, I'm here."

My mouth is full of pastry. "Fimlj otkah" I quickly swallow it down and try again. "I'm okay, thank you. Patrick and I are going to take our time, not rush into anything right away. So, I may have questions, but not tonight." I give her a reassuring smile, hoping she'll let it drop.

"I see." She grimaces. "I hate to be the bearer of bad news, and I'm sure we'll get dragged to a presentation tomorrow, as that's how it usually goes. But, the director frowns pretty heavily on taking things too slowly." I freeze mid-bite, and she continues, "They're going to expect you to track . . . *things* in your fertility app, and you'll be expected to test each month and report results. If you aren't tracking as expected you could be sent for an"—she does finger quotes— "intensive getaway."

My mouth drops open. "Are you serious? It's not enough to marry us off and keep us here, away from our families. They expect to police when and how often we . . ." I trail off, unsure how to process that information. I put my head in my hands.

Faith leans over and puts a hand on my shoulder. "It's going to be okay, Sadie. My fertile week starts soon, but yours doesn't, right? What does your tracker say?" I look to my wrist, where it usually sits.

"I'm not sure exactly, but I think ten days or so?" I'm so used to having it there now, I find myself rubbing the spot absentmindedly.

"See, that's good. You've got a little time to take things slow." She tries to reassure me.

"I mean, they won't *know* if we maybe track something that didn't really happen to keep them off our backs, right? To buy a little more time to ease into things?" I say quietly, not wanting to draw the attention of the hovering staff to our conversation.

Her lips press into a grim line. "Technically, no. But with my first husband Bill, a couple at our honeymoon in Campetán were a ninety percent match, and after their third month they were sent for extra testing when they didn't have results. You two are a ninety-nine percent, right?" I nod. "Yeah, so, I wouldn't want you to have to deal with more tests. Don't put it off too long, okay? Ease into it, sure. But remember the longer you put something off, the more stressful it can feel."

Her look turns compassionate, and I look down at my half-eaten pastry, unable to meet her eyes anymore. I know she's right, and if it weren't for the deception I probably would have no problem taking her advice. Hopefully we're able to work something out before it causes us issues with the director.

"Who's ready to get out of those dresses?" Teddy walks up jangling a room key. I'm surprised to see it's actually a large, antique looking key with a decorative lobster tail attached, instead of an automatic fob like we had back at the NLC.

Patrick is hot on his heels, but simply holds up our key without additional comment. Faith and I both hop up, eager to get out of our gowns. While I was excited to put it on, formal gowns are not exactly comfortable travel wear. The guys lead us down a short hallway filled with nautical décor, and straight out the back door.

"Uhm, guys? Where are we going?" Faith asks.

"You'll see!" Teddy grabs her hand happily and pulls her down a small path through the rocky outcropping towards the sound of the ocean.

"Are we not staying in the main guest house?" I ask, turning to look at Patrick.

"No, actually. It's even better." He gives me a shuttered smile. "I think you'll love it."

The four of us make our way down the path, through some scrubby bushes on a small incline. Just as the ocean sounds peak, we come to the top of the outcropping and the rocky beach spreads before us, bathed in moonlight. I draw in a shocked breath and stop to take in the dazzling view in front of me.

"It's stunning!" I say, awed by the harsh beauty of waves crashing into the rocky beach.

"Yes, you are," Patrick says quietly. I snap my gaze over to where he's standing, drinking me in like I'm going to disappear. I blush, and start moving again. Faith and Teddy are already picking their way along the rocks, and I can see cottages spread along the beachfront.

They stop and wait for us at the first cottage, Faith snuggled into Teddy's side.

"This is us! You guys should be the next one over. Y'all have a good night, and remember"—he looks sternly at Patrick—"if you hurt my sister, they'll never find your body." He pops finger guns at him before turning and leading Faith up to their small cottage.

Oh, my gosh. Really Teddy? I'm mortified, but thankfully Patrick just chuckles in amusement.

"I'm so sorry," I say as we walk to the next cottage.

"It's fine, if I had a baby sister in your shoes, I'd probably say the same thing. He's a good guy, we've talked several times," he confesses.

"What? You two have been talking?" I'm surprised to hear that.

"Yeah, who do you think tipped me off about the hot chocolate?" He nudges me lightly with his elbow, and my mind jumps back to this morning, Charlotte knocking at my door with his thoughtful gift and a steaming mug of cocoa. I hadn't questioned his knowledge at the time, but it makes sense.

"You've really put in a lot of effort, haven't you?" My hand flutters up to touch his mother's hair clip of its own accord. We've arrived in front of our cabin, but instead of heading up he stops and turns to face me, reaching for my hands for the first time since our wedding ceremony.

"Sadie, I know I messed up. I own that, and I apologize. I just hope—" He stops, looks out at the ocean over my shoulder and clears his throat. "I just hope that you'll give me a chance to prove to you that the rest of it wasn't a lie. That I've been me the whole time. The only difference is the last name on the man you chose to marry." He looks back to me and gives my hands a squeeze before letting go and leading the way to our front door.

With the sound of the waves crashing in my ears, I swallow past the lump in my throat and then follow him to our new home—for now.

We wander through the front living space of the cottage, and find ourselves standing inside the master bedroom, staring at an expansive bed taking up most of the cozy space. Patrick steps around the room opening doors, taking note of what's behind them.

This is so awkward. I just want to wash off this day, and sleep. Alone.

Looking down at my massive gown, an unpleasant realization hits me like a brick.

"It looks like the bags are already in the closet. I can shower in the hall bathroom so you'll have some time to yourself in here."

"I'd love to shower, but—" I stop, my throat suddenly dry. "I can't take this dress off without help." I turn, and show him the long row of pearl buttons, which Nell had painstakingly buttoned earlier today.

"Ahh, yes, those would probably be difficult to reach," he says, and runs his hands through his hair with a nervous chuckle. "I can help with that."

I freeze as he steps forward, and starts at the top button. *This is humiliating.*

The warmth of his fingers slowly penetrates the satin fabric of the gown, and I hate myself for feeling a small tingle in response.

Down, girl. We do not get tingles for liars. Even handsome ones with perfect hair.

Patrick continues working down the line of buttons, unaware of my inward battle for indifference. Finally, he reaches the small of my back and the dress sags. I reach up with both hands to hold it in place before spinning out of his reach. "Thank you! That's good, I can take it from here." I give him a grimace, which is as close as I can muster to a smile.

"Of course, happy to help." He walks stiffly over to the closet and grabs a slim black toiletry bag before beating a hasty retreat. The bedroom door closes with a soft click, and my shoulders sag in relief.

This is not how I pictured my wedding night going.

When I wake up the next morning, it takes me a minute to process where I am. The beams overhead are pale and unfamiliar, and my foggy brain slowly recalls that this is our honeymoon beach cottage. I frown, remembering our very non-traditional wedding night before looking over to see that Patrick is already up from the chaise lounge he claimed as his last night. The sheets are neatly folded and stacked at the end, indicating he's been up for a while.

Climbing out of bed, I head to the bathroom and go through my morning routine. There's no sign of Patrick when I emerge, and the house is quiet. As I amble into the kitchen, I smell coffee and spot a wrapped package with a pink frilly bow on the counter. On closer inspection, the tag has my name on it. Well, kind of; it says Sadie O'Roarke. Scowling, I lift the lid off of the box to find my fertility tracking wristband with three spare colored bands.

My eyes roll of their own accord. *Sure, it's way less invasive since you gave me more color options.* Ugh. With a resigned sigh, I select the green band and slide it back onto my wrist. While I tighten the strap so it doesn't flop around, the sound of a door clicking shut catches my attention. I look up and see Patrick, in sweat-plastered workout clothes, coming in the door. His smile is instant, and he shows no signs of being upset about spending his first night as a married man on a couch. I would like to say my stomach didn't tighten at the sight of his shirt clinging to the muscles of his chest, but that would be a lie.

"Good morning!" His voice is chipper. "Did you sleep well?"

"Uhm, yes. How about you? I know the couch in the bedroom is kind of small." Guilt colors my voice, but I firmly remind myself that it's okay to need some space.

"Just fine. I could just barely hear the waves, and I slept like a log." He moves past me to the brimming coffee pot and starts rifling through the white cabinets in search of a mug. On his third cabinet, he finds what he's looking for and turns around with a blue nautical mug which matches the house's décor. He pours a cup and scoops in three heaping spoonfuls of sugar before asking, "Are you hungry?"

"I could eat. Do we have stuff to cook here, or do we have to go back to the guest house?"

"Hmm." he opens the fridge. "It looks like we have the basics. Eggs, some fruit, bacon. Will that work, or would you rather see what they're serving there?"

I think it over and bite my lip. "Let's stay in. It might be kind of awkward running into Teddy and Faith first thing this morning."

"Why, exactly?" He asks with a chuckle.

I shudder. "Because! We know what they've been doing. And they don't know what we *haven't* been doing. Awkward."

His face sobers at the reminder, and he sets eggs and strawberries from the fridge on the counter. "Sadie, there's no reason to feel awkward. I'm sure we are not the only couple in this program who needed a little extra time to get comfortable with each other before jumping in bed. We're taking it slow, remember?"

He leans over and snakes an arm around my waist and gives me a quick side hug and a kiss on the side of my head, and then turns and starts working on breakfast.

"Why don't you let me do that? You look like you might want to shower." I gesture to his workout gear. "Where were you, anyways?" I slide past him and start washing the strawberries.

"Just went for a quick run on the beach. It's beautiful out there! If you wanted, you could come with me tomorrow morning." He waggles his eyebrows at me.

"Patrick, there's a lot we don't know about each other yet, but I think you should at least know that I'm not a morning runner. I'm a morning sleeper."

"Well, you can't blame a man for trying." He snags one of the berries and pops it in his mouth before heading to the shower.

A few minutes later he emerges, just in time to help me dish up our fried eggs, fruit, and toast. We make our way to the built-in kitchen table, which has a bay window overlooking the ocean. I'm savoring my second bite of toast when I hear a chime coming from the front of the house. Patrick and I look at each other, then around to try to locate the source of the noise.

"Do we have a doorbell? I didn't notice last night."

"Probably, but who would be coming to visit us this morning?" He points out the unlikelihood.

We both make our way out of the dining area and I instantly spot the source of the noise—not the doorbell, the television. We've got an appointment in the guest house.

"Ugh, couldn't we at least finish breakfast before they summon us? Don't they know it's early?" I grouch, and head back to the breakfast table.

Patrick sits back down across from me before answering, "It says it's just an introduction meeting, I'm sure it won't be too bad. There are probably some other couples here who we'll get to meet."

That's Patrick, putting a positive spin on things. Doesn't he realize it's too early for that? I reach over and grab my cup of cocoa and give him a return shrug. "We'll see. Faith told me that it's probably for them to lay down some more ground rules."

He looks confused. "Like what? Don't go in the communal swimming pool without a shower? Don't hang your underwear to dry on the porch where everyone can see them?" he jokes, and shovels in another bite of eggs.

"No, like fertility tracker stuff. I hope she's wrong." I trail off, not wanting to delve into the conversation yet.

"Well, it's okay. We can finish our breakfast and then go see what's up," he says reassuringly.

After loading our breakfast dishes into the dishwasher, we head to the guest house for our introduction meeting.

Once we arrive at the guesthouse, we're directed to a small conference room where three couples are already waiting, including Teddy and Faith. We choose seats next to them and exchange quick greetings before an employee makes her way to the front of the room to begin the presentation. She looks to be in her early fifties, with a hint of graying hair around her temples threaded into the blonde.

"Good morning everyone, and thank you so much for rising early on this beautiful day to meet with me! My name is Melissa, and I'm the medical director for this location. I just wanted to go over some specifics with you all to get you started off on the right foot. For those of you who have been here for a while, there won't be any new information, but we always like to give our resident couples a chance to meet." She gestures to the two couples across the table from us, and they all nod or wave in acknowledgement.

"Well then, the very first thing I want to say is that I know this is new to you, but we hope you will see that we here at the Mairmont Honeymoon Resort endeavor to make what could be *uncomfortable* topics for you as normal and painless as possible. We are all here for the same reason—we want to help you start your families!" She fixes us with her best maternal expression. "So please, know that everything we do is to support you so we can work together towards that end. We foster openness and communication between the couples and staff, with the hopes of getting you a baby sooner. Before I get into the nitty gritty, are there any questions?"

When nobody interjects, she launches into her presentation.

An hour later, Melissa leaves us all to mingle. I glance over at Patrick, and he looks as shell-shocked as I feel. Teddy, however, is the first to break the silence.

"Well that was . . . specific," he says bluntly.

One of the men across the table snorts. "You get used to it after the first couple months. They really are matter-of-fact about the whole process, and after a while you will be, too."

"That's good to hear, I guess." He still sounds unsettled, but switches gears to stand and offer his hand. "My name's Teddy

Taylor."

"Hey, Teddy. I'm Emmett Alexander." He stands and shakes Teddy's proffered hand. He's short and stocky, with dark chocolate skin. He gestures to his wife, a petite blonde with bright blue eyes. "This is Carolina."

She gives us all a friendly wave. "Nice to meet you all. We're thrilled to have more company."

"This is Faith, my wife; Sadie, my sister; and Patrick, my new brother-in-law." Teddy points at each of us, and we wave in turn.

"Whoa, brother and sister in the same batch? That's unusual." The taller man across the table chimes in. "I'm Dominic Heath, and this is Odette." He is scruffy, and his relaxed linen clothing looks like he's taken to the beach lifestyle here.

The smile Odette gives us is wan, and I get the distinct impression she doesn't want to be here. She is tall and angular, with flowing black hair. Next to the tiny Carolina, she could be a swan, or a ballerina.

"So, how are you all liking the amenities so far?" Dominic asks.

"It's beautiful here! I went out for a run this morning, and the views are exceptional. I get the feeling that we're pretty secluded here, too," Patrick answers.

"The resort grounds are pretty large, so we've got plenty of privacy, for sure. I asked one of the activity guides and he said there are nearly five hundred acres dedicated to this center, with several thousand surrounding acres of forest," Carolina enthuses.

My mind reels at that number, but I see an opening to dig up more dirt on Josephine. "Oh, I wonder if it's so large due to the pregnancy center being here, also. We heard this was a great honeymoon spot since both are in the same place." I place a hand casually on Patrick's arm.

Carolina nods. "Yep, there's a state-of-the-art medical facility on the grounds. You would have driven past it on your way in. It's the square building with all the windows."

At least we won't have to go far to see Josephine.

"We didn't get in until late, so we probably just missed it," Faith suggests with a friendly smile.

"I wonder if we could get a tour? You know, see where they'll be taking care of us?" I suggest, eager to find Josephine and find out what happened to her after they sedated her and dragged her away. The image of her hanging limp between two guards has been branded into my brain ever since that day.

"Ahh, eager newlyweds I see. Hoping to visit the baby center sooner rather than later." Emmett ribs us with a grin.

Carolina elbows him in the ribs. "Oh, hush. We all started out hopeful that it wouldn't take long. Don't burst their bubbles the first day here! Let them enjoy the possibilities."

The look he gives her speaks of genuine affection, and he slides his arm around her shoulders. "That's my girl, always thinking of others," he says with pride.

Odette snorts delicately and looks out the window, clearly not impressed with the direction of the conversation. Dominic gives her a sideways glance but doesn't try to engage her further.

"Have you four been here awhile?" Faith asks in a delicate tone.

"We've been here about eight months, and we were in the resort at Rico Republica for three months before we transferred here. It was gorgeous down there, but we wanted some cooler weather," Carolina says, nonplussed by the fact that it's been a while.

"Oh, it's almost your anniversary, then! Are you doing anything special to celebrate?" Faith sounds excited by the prospect.

Carolina shrugs. "Probably nothing much. The staff does a really nice dinner whenever someone has an anniversary, so that will be good."

Our attention shifts to Odette and Dominic. When she lets the silence linger beyond comfort, Dominic steps up once again to carry the conversation. "We've been here four months, so not long at all. Are you all just married?" He eyes Faith speculatively, clearly having noted that she's older than the rest of the women here.

Teddy fields that question, "Yes, we're all just in from Georada, but this isn't Faith's first match. It'll be her last match, though." He gives her knee a squeeze, and the look she gives him for that comment says she's downright smitten. I have to look away.

"Overly confident, are we?" Odette's tone is icy as she pins my brother with a glare. "You do know that despite the supposed superior genetic matching," she does air quotes, "there are no guarantees. You two might not even be that good of a genetic match, just the best available."

It's clear she has a chip on her shoulder, but Teddy doesn't let it faze him. "Actually, we're a ninety-nine percent match. So, we have an exceptionally good shot. Were you two not as high as you'd hoped?" It's his turn to pin her with a no-nonsense look.

She is the first to break the staring contest and drops her eyes to her lap where her hands are tightly clenched. Dominic tries to set his hand on top of hers, but she flinches away from him and stands, striding out of the room without a look back.

I can feel my eyebrows trying to climb straight off my forehead as I look back at Dominic, his shoulders slumped.

"Things aren't going well, I take it?" Patrick says, his tone gentle.

"It's not your fault, man. Just keep trying. She'll come around," Emmett says, and gives him a firm slap on the back.

Based on what I just saw, that's wildly unlikely. But that wouldn't be helpful to tell Dominic.

"It's my own fault. I shouldn't have told her about Carla. We were already not doing well, and from that moment on she's completely iced me out. Nothing I say makes a difference." He drops his head into his hands heavily.

"Who's Carla?" I ask.

He looks up, a weary expression on his scruffy face. "She was my sweetheart back home. We dated through high school and signed up together when she had to join the program. We both got sent to the local New Life Center together, and we really thought we'd been matched. But, it turns out that she'd matched some guy from Ionoiri. And I matched Odette. It was torture watching each other date somebody else, and I made the mistake of telling her that we'd signed up in hopes of matching each other. I was her only match, and we're only fifty-five percent. So she feels like she's wasting her time with me, but there's nothing we can do about it. It's going to be a long freaking three years." He sounds utterly dejected, and I can't say I blame him. That's a bad hand if ever I heard one.

"Where are Carla and her match?" I ask gently.

His face is grim when he looks up to answer, "They are already in Ionoiri, at the pregnancy center. She got pregnant two months ago, but she's not doing so well."

Emmett gives him another slap on the back in camaraderie, and the rest of us exchange glances.

"I'm so sorry to hear that, Dominic. Hopefully, she'll be fine, and the next thing you hear will be good news." I offer my most encouraging smile, but it falls flat.

"Thanks, I hope so."

Carolina suggests a group beach walk to continue getting to know each other, so we all tromp along the beach until lunch, when we go our separate ways. We spend the rest of the afternoon in our cabin reading. Patrick seems lighter now that his secret isn't between us anymore. He reads half of a military space adventure novel before I'm through a few chapters of my favorite western romance, which I can't seem to focus on. My distracted brain loops back over the same page every time I stop to sneak a peek at my handsome, but untrustworthy, husband. My mind keeps turning over the dichotomy that is Patrick. One of the worst parts of this situation is that, now, I can't trust my own judgment. Can I learn to trust him again?

Can I learn to trust myself again?

THREE

COLD SHOWER

Another day dawns, and this time I sit up in bed and look over to see a rumpled Patrick, still awkwardly stuffed onto the chaise lounge in our room. The light sounds of his breathing can barely be heard over the waves outside. *That does not look comfortable.* His neck is twisted to fit, and his ankles and feet are dangling over the end of the dark blue leather cushion. *I'm going to have to let him in the bed tonight.* The thought makes my throat tighten, but it's not fair to him to keep him squashed onto that tiny lounge chair.

He interrupts my train of thought by trying to roll to his back, only to clear the edge and flail his arm wildly before hitting the ground with a thud. His groan echoes around our room.

"Are you okay? Need a hand up?" I toss the words down to him.

His voice is gravelly when he answers, "Why is it the one morning you're actually awake is the one I fall off this thing?" He pops the side of the offending furniture with a clenched fist from his position on the wood floor.

I climb out of the very fluffy mattress and walk around to offer him a hand. "Come on, time to get up."

He's stretched out, hands propping his head up from the cold floor. That pose has really got his biceps popping out of his sleep shirt. It's also making that sleep shirt ride up just a little from his pajama pants, and it takes all my willpower not to check out his exposed stomach. *Remember, you're still mad at him. Even if he is a tasty-looking stud muffin.*

"Okay, but this is the first time I've been flat in almost forty-eight hours." He extends one hand, and I wrap both of mine around it and pull him to his feet.

"Thanks, Sadie." He leans down and gives me a soft kiss on the top of my head before padding into the bathroom. The door shuts with a soft click, and I head into the hall bath.

A short while later we're both dressed and ready to head down for breakfast at the guest house. We made plans yesterday to meet Faith and Teddy there, and then do a tour of the medical facility right after. I'm excited to finally see Josephine, and also curious what this top of the line facility entails.

We made our way down the beach in companionable silence, and we're the first ones in the dining hall for breakfast. A pink-shirted waiter brings around a basket of delicious pastries, and I've already finished a cheese Danish and started on a cherry turnover by the time Teddy and Faith walk in, nearly ten minutes late.

"What took you two so long?" I grump around a mouthful of flaky cherry goodness.

Patrick snorts next to me, and for the first time I take in Faith's slightly mussed hair and reddened cheeks.

"Oh, nothing much. Just overslept," Teddy says as he holds her chair out for her, and she gives him a beaming smile. "So, what's on the menu this morning?"

We all order way too much food and discuss what activities we want to do when we're done with the medical tour. The guys want to go sailing, and also go out on a lobster boat. Faith and I want to go hike to a rocky outpoint with an old lighthouse. It's been out of use for well over a hundred years, as there's almost no marine traffic to this area anymore, but they have maintained it for visitors.

We're only allowed one outing per day, so by the time we finish our breakfast smorgasbord, we've got the entire week planned.

Even if it's awkward at times, I'm so glad Teddy and Faith are here with us. *At some point I'm going to have to tell them about Patrick.* My mood darkens at the thought. Not today. Maybe later this week when we're not in earshot of so many employees. A quick glance around the room and I count no less than six pink-shirted men lingering. Finished with our planning and extravagant breakfast, the mood is light as we head out the front door to the medical center for our tour.

The driveway is very different in the daytime, as we can now see that it's planted down both sides with tall decorative grass bunches which blow in the continuous breeze, and long-stalked flowers that bob brightly interspersed among them. The four of us make a pretty jovial group, and in no time we're walking in the front doors of the medical facility. Melissa, the director, is waiting for us in the lobby. Her outfit today is flamingo pink scrubs, paired with chunky shoes covered in rainbows. It's a polar opposite vibe than Dr. Mitch gave off, and I'm relieved about that. As we approach, a cloud of her floral perfume engulfs us.

"Welcome newlyweds! We're so excited to show you all around our dedicated pregnancy and fertility center! You four are actually the first to ever request a tour, but we like the idea so much that we're going to put it on the activity menu from now on. Why not get comfortable here, even before the big positive?" She says it as if it's the most novel idea that she's ever heard. Her smile seems genuine, and I can feel a release of tension I didn't know I was holding in my shoulders.

"Who's ready to get started?" She looks at us eagerly, and once we all nod she bustles towards a shiny white hallway with a big pink stripe down the center of the walls. "Here on the main floor, we have our basic appointment rooms. This is where we see you for any ordinary medical visits, confirm pregnancy tests, and even perform ultrasounds." She stops at the open door for a pretty standard-looking appointment room. The only difference is the huge screen built into one wall, and an assortment of medical wands that come out of the wall.

"This is the ultrasound equipment, and the high resolution scans are projected directly onto the wall. You can actually see the baby *bigger* than life size—can you imagine? One day, with any luck, you four will be here checking out your little nuggets on that very screen." She sighs dreamily before continuing down the hallway. "At this end of the hallway we have a full barrage of screening equipment. So, if we don't see results in the timeframe we'd expect, we are able to assess any issues right here in house. I have to say, you chose the best honeymoon location." She stops, puffing her chest slightly with pride, "You can have anything you need on your fertility journey taken care of right here, while still staying in the comfort of your own perfect ocean-front bungalow."

She leads us up a flight of stairs, and on the second floor there is a baby blue stripe down the walls. "This floor houses all of our second-tier pregnancy support services. If you need some extra help or monitoring, we have suites on this floor where you can stay and receive round the clock care. However, the designers have really gone all out to make each room feel more like it's at a spa than a medical facility." This time, the door she stops at is open to a pristine and calming turquoise green room with a large bed in the center, and antique lanterns studding the walls. The attached bathroom has a massive infinity tub in front of floor-to-ceiling windows which overlook a thick thatch of woods. You could almost miss the medical panel and tubing recessed into the wall behind the bed, if you weren't looking for it.

"Uhm, is there a way to cover those windows when you're in here? It's beautiful, but I don't usually show all my business to whoever might be walking by." Faith gestures up and down her body nervously.

"Of course! The windows are fully adjustable for privacy." She walks to the corner, and with the press of a button the windows fog fully, with one more press they fog only halfway up so you can still see out, and on the third press they resume their crystal-clear state. "There's also a nightlight function which will cause it to glow." Her answer is chipper.

"It seems like they've thought of everything," I say. "Are there any pregnant women on the floor now?"

She shakes her head sadly. "No, not right now. Every pregnancy is big news around here, so we usually deck out the hallways with balloons whenever someone is in.

"Oh, okay," I say, confusion coloring my tone.

Her brow furrows. "Were you expecting someone?"

How to answer without giving away Glitch's illicit research? My mind spins before answering, "Not necessarily. A friend of ours was supposed to be honeymooning here, but we didn't see her at the introduction yesterday, and I hoped she might have been here." I give her a smile, silently praying she'll let it drop.

"Oh, I understand. Right now we have four couples at this location, and unfortunately no babies yet this year. Hopefully you four will be able to change that soon." She pauses, and looks around as if someone is going to jump out of the woodwork before whispering, "Between you and me, I've reviewed your files and you four have *exceptionally* strong genetic match potential. The best I've seen in my entire five years at this facility, so we've all got high hopes for you in the next few months." Her eyes twinkle with excitement, but my stomach churns at her words.

I force myself to paste on a smile, and not think of Patrick sleeping on a too-small chaise lounge. Faith thankfully speaks up. "Oh, we've got high hopes ourselves. Teddy is my third match, and I'd love to finally have my baby." Her voice chokes up at the end, and I can tell she's fighting back tears. Teddy wordlessly slips his arm around her shoulders and pulls her into his side.

The blatant display of hope makes me feel ashamed of myself. Here I am, miserable and feuding with Patrick, a ninety-nine percent genetic match for me, while Faith has been married and divorced from two men before Teddy and still hasn't been able to conceive. When I think about how lucky I am, how hard she's had to fight for what's been handed to me, it makes me reconsider my reluctance to start a family. I look over at Patrick, who's been silent for this entire tour to find him studying me intently.

We lock eyes, and the moment fills with tension. His hand flutters up, as if he wants to touch me, but hesitates and he lowers it back down without making contact. I glance away and clear my throat, not willing to have this moment in front of an audience.

You have to talk to him soon, Sadie. And Teddy and Faith, for that matter. My stern pep-talk does little to encourage me.

"Okay! If you're ready to continue the tour, the top floor is the most exciting yet!" She says, oozing enthusiasm as she hustles out the door and back down the hallway to the stairwell. We climb another flight of stairs, this time coming out on a landing with a butter yellow stripe on the walls.

"This floor is where the magic happens!" She flings her hands wide as if, instead of another hallway, we're looking out over a majestic view. She leads us to the first doorway on the right. "Each room on this hallway is a delivery and maternal care suite. This is where you'll come for the last month of your pregnancy, stay for delivery, and two to four weeks after the baby's born for round-the-clock monitoring."

She may intend that to sound safe and inviting, but instead, it makes me feel like the walls are closing in. Living as a bug under a microscope for nearly two months sounds like a circle of hell. And if I remember correctly, my sister-in-law Tess was miserable towards the end of both her pregnancies. Why would they keep us locked up in this tower? I'm about to ask as much when Teddy interjects.

"We don't actually have to stay though, right? We were under the impression that once our pregnancy is confirmed and the first trimester is over, we'd be able to go home to Georada to be with family."

She hesitates, and for the first time her chipper façade slips. "Well, technically no, you don't have to stay in all scenarios."

I stiffen, knowing there's a "but" coming.

"But, we only release pregnant mothers on a case-by-case basis. Many find it better to stay here until after the baby is born, so they can be monitored and have medical attention available twenty-four-seven. And depending on your individual risk profile, it may be required."

My jaw drops. The NLC training courses they'd made us take at the beginning of this had explicitly stated that after a healthy first trimester, we'd all get to go home to see our families. If my stomach was churning before, now it feels like I swallowed fire ants. Hot bile rises up the back of my throat, and I turn on my heel and head straight for the stairs. I keep my eyes locked on the floor, hoping no one stops me before I can make it outside. Tears blur my vision by the time I see a baby blue stripe, and when my sneaker-clad feet hit the last step, which puts me back on the pink floor, tears have started to escape the corners of my eyes.

I rush to the end of the hall, straight out the door, and descend the front steps, head down to hide my overflowing tears. With no destination in mind except *away*, I let my feet lead me to the rocky beach outcropping behind the guest house. Sawgrasses taller than my head sway, but I can't hear the swishing of their blades over the rushing in my ears. I stumble down the boardwalk, and my feet crunch on the pebbles but I still don't stop. Looking left, I spot our cabins. So I head right, towards the empty stretch of beach, and I just walk. Tears stream down my face freely now that I'm alone, and if any sobs escape me, they are torn away by the ocean wind that relentlessly whips my face.

I don't know how long I walk in the cold, leaning into the wind with the dark, stormy ocean waves as my only company. Eventually, I stumble, and rocks bite painfully into my palms and knee, right through my jeans. I gingerly slide back to a sitting position and examine my palms. They're sore, but not bleeding. My left knee, on the other hand, has a gash that is bleeding down my shin. I press a palm across it to staunch the bleeding, and stare out at the waves, their tumultuous show fitting my solemn demeanor.

After a few minutes, the tears stop. My mind is finally blank, numbed by the sea, the wind, and the solitude. The blood has stopped rushing in my ears, and my knee still looks ugly but has clotted for now. *That's going to suck to clean,* I think absently, before hearing rocks grinding together behind me. I turn, expecting a bird or something, and see Patrick sitting a ways up the beach, watching me without intruding on my private moment. He must have shifted and caused some rocks to slide down.

He lifts a hand and gives me a small wave. I wave back, and he holds up one of my hoodies in offering. The gesture causes me to self-assess and realize that I am, in fact, freezing. I nod and start to stand, but he pops up and jogs over to me before I attempt to stand with my sore knee. I take his extended hand, and he pulls me to my feet.

"I'm sorry, I didn't mean to disturb you. My foot fell asleep, and when I moved, the rocks slid," he says, looking bashful.

"It's okay. How long have you been out here?" I take the jacket from him, and gratefully slide it over my tousled hair, sighing as the warmth engulfs me.

"Well, I was right behind you when you left the tour. But when you turned away from the cabin, I jogged over and got your jacket before I caught back up with you a mile or so back. I thought it would be best if you weren't completely alone, since you seemed so upset." He shrugs one shoulder.

"Well, thank you for bringing my jacket. I didn't realize how cold I was until I saw it." I rub my hands together, trying to get the blood to flow back to my chilled digits.

"Are you ready to walk back? We should probably take it slow —that knee looks like it hurts." He frowns, concern etching his handsome face. "Are you *able* to walk back? I can carry you if you need me to."

I wave a hand, dismissing his concerns. "I'm fine, but yes, let's head back."

I appreciate the fact that he doesn't push me to talk, he just lets me be. We make our way slowly back towards the cabin, the wind at our backs in this direction. I stumble, and his hand wraps around my elbow before I can hit the ground again. Once I'm steady, he lets go, and I instantly miss the warmth of his grip.

"I'm sorry for dragging you out here. It was all too much, the thought of being stuck in one of those rooms for months, constantly monitored . . ." I trail off, unsure how to describe the feeling without sounding crazy. I clear my throat. "I'm used to a lot more freedom, back home. First they want us to track every intimate detail of our personal lives, and now they say they may not allow us to go home, even when we are having the baby." A lump rises in my throat, and I have to swallow twice before I can continue. "I can't imagine having a baby here, surrounded by medical staff, a thousand miles from home. I always thought I'd be back in Jackson Flats, with my mom and Tess, and able to take the baby home the next day. Being isolated and alone here feels like I'm no different than a monkey in a cage." I look out over the waves, my arms tightly crossed over my chest.

"I understand why you feel that way. I don't want to be this far from family when our child is born, either." His voice comes out in a low, soothing murmur.

I shake my head, anger still coursing through me in hot waves.

He stops, turns to me and holds me gently by both arms. "Sadie, I promise you, right here, right now, that I will do *everything* in my power to make sure you get to go home." One hand drifts up, and he gently pulls a strand of my chestnut hair back from where the wind whipped it into my face.

I look up at him, and I'm sure he can see my troubled thoughts in my eyes. His expression is tense, and I can see the muscle tick in his jaw.

His thumb swipes down my cheek, and over my lip, soft as a whisper. My reaction is involuntary, lips parting of their own accord at his touch—both comforting and searing. My thoughts scatter, the anger sucked away in the icy wind.

"I wish I knew what you were thinking right now." His voice is still soft, almost a warm purr in my ear. His thumb skates down the side of my neck, over my frantic pulse, teasing me.

I feel myself sway towards him once, twice. His other hand slides down my arm, to entwine his fingers with my own. "We should head back and get that knee taken care of." He gives my neck one last soft stroke, and then releases me so we can start the long trek back.

I stare at my reflection in the bathroom mirror, steam fogging the air around me from my long soak in the tub. My hair is tied back in a French braid, and I'm wearing a simple plaid pajama set. *Not what I envisioned wearing on a honeymoon, but, hey, if the pajamas fit.* My teeth are brushed, I've slathered on my lotion, and there is nothing else to do in this bathroom to keep me here. I'm stalling, and I know it. I arch one eyebrow and give myself my sternest face in the mirror.

"Sadie, you face down angry steers, and wrangle fifteen-hundred-pound horses on a daily basis back home. One single man, who you are married to, is not something you should be scared of. Get your plaid-pajama-clad butt in gear and go tell him he doesn't have to spend another night on that chaise lounge." I give myself a quiet pep-talk, but it makes me feel silly more than motivated. I huff out a breath.

That's it, I'm done being ridiculous. Turning, I sweep open the door, and a rush of steam escapes into the colder bedroom. Patrick looks up from a book, already settled for the night on the chaise lounge. His ankles and feet dangle off, but the wave he gives me is friendly before he looks down and continues reading.

It would be a lot easier to stay mad at him if he were a surly jerk. Walking to the end of the bed, I perch lightly, and fidget with the end of my braid. After a moment, he realizes that I'm sitting there and looks up expectantly.

"Is everything okay? Do you need me to look at your knee again?" he asks.

He'd thoroughly cleaned and bandaged my knee for me, after we'd gotten back from our walk. I already re-bandaged it after I got out of the tub, though.

"No, my knee is fine. Thank you for your help, though." I hesitate, biting my lip, unsure where to start. He sits up and holds his place with his finger, giving me his full attention. His gray sleep shirt is rumpled, and so is his hair. It's messy and endearing, and were it not for this awkwardness between us, I would reach over and smooth it out with my fingers. I bet it's soft.

"Are you sure everything's all right? You can tell me if it's not, I won't be upset."

His question jolts me from my train of thought, and I feel the blush as it overtakes my cheeks. "Yes, it is. In fact, I wanted to talk to you about you sleeping in the bed tonight." I pat the mattress next to me in an exaggerated manner.

"O-kay . . ." He seems surprised.

"I know things are still awkward between us, and I'm not suggesting we put anything physical on the table. It's just, I can tell you're uncomfortable sleeping over there, and this bed has plenty of room to share. I feel really selfish making you sleep on that tiny chair when I'm hogging the whole bed." The words tumble out of me in a rush.

He smiles warmly at me. "Sadie, that's really generous of you, but I volunteered to sleep over here until you get more comfortable. Are you sure this is what you want? I really am fine."

"Yes, I'm sure. There's no way you're comfortable, and you literally fell off that thing this morning and landed on the floor." The words come out steady and self-assured, and I mentally pat myself on the back.

"Okay, then. If you're sure, I'll join you. Can I ask you one favor, though?"

"Sure, what is it?"

"Can we switch sides? I want to take the side closest to the door."

"Uhm, okay. Yeah, that's fine." I wasn't expecting the question, but I don't care which side I sleep on.

Grabbing my charger and mini-tablet off the side table, I walk around to the other side and plug it back in.

"Is there something magical about that side that makes you sleep better?" I joke, trying to break the tension I feel as I slip under the covers.

He slides in next to me, and his face is serious when he answers. "Well, if there is another kidnapping attempt, they'll most likely be coming through the door. So I'd prefer to be between you and them if at all possible."

"Oh." I pull the covers up, and stare at the ceiling for a long moment. "Do you really think that's likely? They didn't succeed at the NLC, and there weren't any more attempts while we were there."

"Unfortunately, I do. There were two more attempts while we were still at the NLC, but none of them made it past the increased guard force. I know this location was notified to increase its security staff, but better safe than sorry." His mouth is pressed into a grim line.

I don't even try to hide my shock. "There were two more attempts? Seriously? Why is this the first I'm hearing about it?"

He turns on his side to face me, and props himself up on one elbow. "This is the first I've heard of it, too. I sent a message to Glitch this afternoon to ask him to do some more digging since Josephine wasn't here in the medical facility. He called me back while you were bathing and mentioned the two additional kidnapping attempts. Apparently, they didn't make it past the exterior guard force, so they didn't notify the inside personnel. We both found that sketchy, so I'm not taking any chances, even with the small details."

My stomach feels like I swallowed a rock at that information. "So, did he find out where Josephine is?"

He shakes his head. "Unfortunately no. There are no transfer records in her file. The last record was of a blood test confirming the pregnancy was still progressing, and it was recorded under this location two days ago."

"That makes no sense. Do you think they lied on the tour today about the floor being empty? Or where the heck is she, if not in the medical facility?" The thought is troubling. Either they've lost a pregnant woman, or they're hiding one—neither is good.

"Right now, we don't know. Glitch is going to keep digging, and hopefully you and I can keep digging without raising any alarm bells. He promised to call as soon as he sees or hears anything else pop up on her record."

"Well, thank you for calling him. Hopefully we'll get to the bottom of it soon. Something is not right here."

He squeezes my hand before releasing me. "I agree. We'll get to the bottom of this, one way or another."

With that, he reaches over and turns off the light.

FOUR

COUPLE'S MASSAGE

T he next week passes in an activity-filled blur. Patrick and I are in an unspoken truce, and I can feel myself starting to thaw towards him day by day. It's hard to stay mad when he's so genuine. He is the same man I fell for at the NLC, and my heart is slowly accepting that. I think it's time to let Teddy and Faith know the truth, too.

Today we're all hiking out to the old lighthouse. Patrick and Teddy both have small packs on their backs with lunch supplies. Once we stop for lunch, I'm going to tell them. Or make Patrick tell them, since it's his secret.

The guys are a few yards ahead, and Faith is trekking along beside me quietly. Perhaps too quietly.

"Everything okay today, Faith? I thought we were both excited about this hike, but your heart doesn't seem to be in it."

She gives me a thin smile, with none of her usual boundless cheer. "Yes, I'm fine. Today was the start of my pregnancy testing cycle." Her voice grows thick. "It was negative, of course. I know it's still early, really early, so it could be positive in a few days. But after a while, you start to feel like it's *always* going to be negative." She trails off, and I can tell how badly she's hurting. "Teddy has given me hope again, Sadie. It's dangerous.

What if I really set my heart on it happening this time, and instead I'm right back where I started, again?"

We stop in the middle of the trail, and I give her my best sister hug. She clings to me tightly, and over her shoulder I see the guys continuing on, blissfully unaware as they chatter about whatever they're pointing to in the trees. I pull back a little, but she's still holding me tightly, so I pull her back. We stay like that for a long moment before I decide what I should say.

"Faith, there are no guarantees in this world. I think you and I are both really clear on that, at this point of our lives." I choose my words carefully, "But your endless hope, your determination to be happy regardless of your life circumstances . . . Those are the things that I love about you. You are more than just your mothering potential to me. I hope that you can see that about yourself. I don't believe the tests will always be negative—but even if they were, I would *still* have chosen you for my sister. Because you are so much more as a person than your ability to spit out another human."

Her grip around me becomes almost painful for a second, before she eases up. I can feel her shoulders shaking, and I make soft soothing sounds while patting her on the back. At some point, the guys realized we were no longer behind them and came back, and they're waiting for us a few yards away.

When she's ready and her tears have subsided, she pulls back and wipes under her eyes a few times. She sniffles. "Thank you, Sadie. I didn't know how much I needed to hear that from someone until you said it." She squares her shoulders. "Let's get back to this hike, shall we?" She offers her elbow to me with an exaggerated flourish.

I take her elbow, but don't budge yet. "There's one more thing. Have you talked to Teddy about how you're feeling?"

Her gaze drops to the leaf-strewn trail with guilt. "Not really, no. We're still in the honeymoon phase, and this is all so new to him. I don't want to be the black cloud that rains all over him, when he's still getting started."

I nod, as that's exactly what I suspected. "Faith, you need to know something about the Taylor family. It's very important."

She looks confused now. "What's that?"

"We are as tough as they come, and we are loyal to a fault. I know that you are coming fresh off a bad relationship . . ." I don't even say her ex's name, because I don't want to bring his harmful attitudes to this beautiful fall day. "But, you should know that when Teddy committed to you, he went all in. Just like I did for Patrick. We Taylors don't take marriage lightly, and however this shakes out, Teddy will be there for you. I know my brother well enough to know that, and I also know that he wouldn't want you hurting in silence. When you're ready, you should try to talk to him."

Leaving her with that to think on, I start down the path to catch up to the guys. I try not to think too hard about my own words regarding Patrick, because I'm still not ready to look that closely at my own feelings. *One thing at a time, Sadie.*

Once we reach the spot where Teddy and Patrick are waiting, I release her elbow. Teddy instantly wraps an arm around her shoulders and pulls her in for a tender kiss on the forehead.

"Everything okay, honey?" He looks her over as if the problem will magically present itself in writing.

I snort, and he looks up.

"What's so funny?"

"I love you, but you're dumb sometimes. Come on, Patrick, let's give them some space. Maybe we can find a good place to stop for lunch." I charge down the trail, knowing the only solution for Teddy and Faith is some one-on-one honesty.

Patrick follows without question until we've rounded a bend in the trail a few minutes later. "Everything okay?" he asks, his voice breaking the wooded stillness.

"Not really, but it will be." I give him a reassuring smile. "I wanted to talk to you about something, though."

"Anything. What's up?" his tone is light, but I can hear the worry underneath.

"I think it's time we tell Teddy and Faith who you are. I don't want to keep it from them, and it would be nice to have someone in the know to talk to."

His mouth is set in a grim line, and he's silent for a few more minutes as we walk amongst the towering, red-and-gold-leaved trees. To my surprise, when he speaks next, he doesn't argue—despite his obvious reservation.

"Okay, we can tell them." He sounds resigned.

Stopping, I spin to face him. "Are you sure? I know it's a big deal for you. We can talk about it more if you want."

"Yes, I'm sure. I appreciate your honesty, and your desire to be upfront with your family. You're already keeping this from the rest of the world—I won't ask you to change who you are to keep my secret from them, too," he says, jaw set in determination.

I roll what he said over in my mind, taking in the weight of it. I hadn't thought about it before now, but he's right. We are living as the O'Roarkes currently, which is neither my nor his legal name. Part of me accepted that because I wasn't ready to tell anyone else that he'd duped me. But part of me wasn't willing to dive into the political ramifications of who he really is. *It's easier to pretend to be an O'Roarke than to be a Royce.* Guilt washes over me when I realize that I've been enjoying the benefits of the same deception I'd wanted to crucify him for.

"I think I owe you an apology, Patrick." My voice comes out low, humbled.

His eyebrows shoot up. "What? Why would you owe me an apology?" He crosses the divide between us, invading my personal space. He reaches up and smooths a piece of wayward brunette hair back from my face, and my stomach flip-flops.

My mouth has gone suddenly dry, so I have to swallow before I can answer him. "Well, I was so angry at you for not telling me who you really were—and I do think that was justified anger—but, I turned around and slipped right into it with you, and never even realized that I was being a hypocrite. I've only been a Royce for, what, a week and a half?"

I look up at him, and he gives me a single tense nod, but doesn't interrupt me.

"The pressure I feel from your family's political position is huge, and I've only been part of the family for a short time. Nobody even knows who I am, or cares. But you . . . this is your whole life. Your whole future, and the expectations of an entire *continent* of people." I pause, the weight settling more fully in my mind. "I guess I understand more now why you wanted to be free of that for a while. And I'm sorry I judged you for that decision." I look up, and his face is so serious, I can't tell what he's thinking.

The moment drags on, until I can't take it anymore. "Would you say something, please?"

He doesn't speak, but he does wrap his hand around the back of my head, and pulls me in for a sudden, fierce kiss. I freeze at first, unsure, but after a moment I relax into his hard chest, my hands softly resting against his warmth. He backs me up, and I feel the rough bark of a tree lightly against my back. Letting go of my head, he brackets me in with both arms between him and the trunk, and after a moment pulls back, resting his forehead against mine.

My lips are tingling, and my brain is blank from the sudden display of passion. At some point, I'd clenched a hand into the soft fabric of his t-shirt, pulling him in closer, and I force myself to let it go, but leave my hand pressed to him where I can feel his heart pounding.

His voice is rough with emotion when he finally says, "Thank you, Sadie. Thank you for understanding," and then he crushes me to his chest in a bear hug. I hug him back and close my eyes to soak in the moment, my own heart pounding to match his.

A throat clears, and both of us pop our heads up. "You have an interesting definition of 'finding a lunch spot.' " Teddy quips, an amused note in his voice.

Patrick steps back, but instead of releasing me, he slips an arm down around my waist, holding me lightly against his side. "Well, we *are* newlyweds, what do you expect?" he jokes, giving no hint of the tension that was simmering between us seconds ago.

"Yeah, yeah. Still my baby sister, so, keep it to yourself." Teddy waves dismissively, and Faith elbows him in the ribs.

"Ignore him. Did you find a spot to eat?" She seems lighter, and I hope that means she confided in Teddy, but I won't meddle and push it further either way.

"Yep, right over there." Patrick points to a nice, clear spot I hadn't noticed.

"Perfect!" Faith drags Teddy by the hand, and he shakes his head at her enthusiasm.

After we've set out the blanket and all helped ourselves to our lunch feast, I give Patrick an encouraging sideways glance. He's just taken a huge bite of a deviled egg and gives me a shrug. I giggle at his goofiness. *It's nice to see he has a relaxed and silly side, too.*

Our lighthearted moment is interrupted by sudden music blaring from Patrick's pocket.

"What the heck?" he mumbles around a half-chewed deviled egg as he tries to dig his mini-tablet from his pocket.

Before he succeeds, however, the green band on my wrist starts buzzing so aggressively it feels like it's going to shake my hand off my wrist. "Oh, my word!" I flip my wrist up, to see what's going on. My good mood vanishes, and my stomach falls straight to my feet. There, on my wristband are two blinking, entwined pink hearts.

Patrick manages to kill the music coming from his phone. "What was that, the cha-cha?"

I drop my still-buzzing wrist to my lap, the plate of delicious picnic food abandoned. I can't believe I forgot. *Fertile Week.* After a minute or so, the buzzing stops. I feel physically rattled by the experience, and I can't believe it's going to do that every month—it's so obnoxious.

Patrick is still looking at his phone, and hasn't realized that I've checked out. "Huh, there are hearts on here. Why would it give me a heart alarm?" He clicks it. "Oh, it says—OH." He finally looks up and sees my horrified expression. He glances over at Teddy and Faith. The pity on Faith's face is plain, but Teddy chuckles.

"Mortifying, isn't it? Let's announce it to the whole world!" Teddy shakes his head in derision. "These people do not understand subtlety. Or privacy, for that matter."

"Can we change the subject?" I blurt, wanting to pretend it never happened. *Good luck with that, when the medical director wants to know why you didn't track any extracurricular activities.*

"Sure, what do you want to talk about?" Faith jumps in to rescue me.

"How much further away is this lighthouse, anyways? We've been hiking almost two hours," Patrick asks.

"Not far, I think another half mile or so. But if you don't want to finish the hike, we can all turn around, or the two of us can finish and you two could head back early . . ." she trails off.

"Nope, we're good. Can't wait to keep hiking!" My voice sounds high-pitched, even to me.

Teddy raises a single eyebrow and takes me in without a word. Faith bites her lip worriedly. Patrick reaches over, and places a hand gently on my arm, steadying me.

"I agree, can't wait to see the lighthouse." He picks my plate up, and hands it back to me. "But first, we need to eat this delicious lunch so we don't have to carry it anymore. What do you think they put in these deviled eggs, anyways?"

"I'd wager paprika, and enough cayenne to remind you of the hellfire they came from." Teddy pops one into his mouth whole.

I roll my eyes but am inwardly grateful to move on.

FIVE

FERTILE WEEK

F our hours later we walk back through the door of our cottage tired, sunburnt, and with a few new blisters apiece. The lighthouse was beautiful, and the view from the top was postcard-worthy. But the enjoyment wasn't there for me when *fertile week* kept running through my panicked brain on repeat the entire time. Patrick and I are just starting to get on better footing, but that doesn't mean I'm ready to jump into bed, even if he is a knee-melting kisser. *I wonder what he's expecting now. Is he ready to take things to the next level, even though I'm not?*

Patrick, blissfully unaware of my mental laps, drops the backpack off right inside the door and takes an exaggerated stretch which causes his chest muscles to flex impressively. I stare for a moment at the mesmerizing motion before heading to the kitchen, looking for a distraction. I don't make it, though, because our blinking television display catches my eye.

The entire screen is blinking an obnoxious, bubblegum pink message.

Today is a very special day! It's the beginning of your first fertile week here at Mairmont Honeymoon Resort. To commemorate this special time here with us, celebratory dinner and drinks will be catered to your cottage each evening. Additionally, all of your activities have automatically been pushed back five days to accommodate more time together. Good luck, and have fun!

The little kissy face at the end of that message makes me want to punch something. The message is pretty clear. Stay in, and get busy. Ugh.

Patrick walks up beside me, and takes in the flashing screen. "Do you think it's going to stay like that for five whole days? The blinking is awful." He holds his hand up to block the glare, and makes an exaggerated squinty face.

"I certainly hope not, or we're going to have to abandon the living room. Especially since they *so kindly* cancelled all activities, and our ability to leave for dinner." I can hear the anger rising in my own voice, and try again to tamp it down. *What did you expect, Sadie? The whole point of this place is to get you knocked up.*

He puts a hand on my shoulder, but I flinch back, and he withdraws it, furrowing his eyebrows. "Is everything okay?"

I shrug and cross my arms, not even sure how to begin a conversation that says, "Hey, I know we're starting to patch things up, but you should still stay on *your* side of the bed, 'kay?"

After I'm silent for another long while, he tries again. "Is this about fertile week? Because I think we need to sit down and talk about that."

I still don't answer, instead I head straight into the kitchen. It may not be *my* kitchen back home, but it's still familiar territory. When in doubt, bake. I start rummaging through the fridge and pull out eggs and butter before moving to the pantry and grabbing all my dry goods. This kitchen has a sleek blue stand mixer in the corner, and I can't wait to get a little flour on it.

I locate the paddle attachment and get the oven preheating in silence while I wait for the microwave to beep, signaling that the butter has been softened to the perfect point. Then, on autopilot, I begin creaming up the butter and brown sugar. I hear a bar stool scrape against the wooden floor over the whirring of the mixer as Patrick pulls it out, but I don't turn to face him. Instead, I brace both hands on the cool stone countertop, and watch the butter and sugar dance around the shiny bowl. Once the butter is light as a cloud, I crack and add the eggs one at a time. I turn it off to scrape down and begin adding my dry ingredients. I quickly measure and add them all, and with one more quick whiz around the mixer, the cookie dough is ready.

My movements are calm and practiced as I scoop out perfectly portioned globs of dough onto the baking sheet. Once I slide it onto the middle rack and start the timer, I finally turn to face Patrick. Somehow, I find I can't quite meet his eyes, so I guess his hands will have to do. They're relaxed, strong, and lying on the countertop. He's not a man that fidgets, and I appreciate that about him.

"Sadie, I really wish you'd talk to me," he starts. "But if you won't, can I tell you what I'm thinking? You can chime in when you're ready."

I glance up to see his sincere gaze before quickly dropping my eyes again, and nod.

"I think we both know that we're not ready to take things to the next level yet."

Tension I didn't know I'd been holding in my shoulders starts to drain away at those words.

"However, we still need to decide how we want to handle the expectations of the medical director. They fully expect us to be tracking some things this week, and while I find that ludicrous, we can't do much about that at the moment." This time I look up and lock eyes with him.

He finds it ridiculous, too? The smile he gives me is warm, and this time when he reaches across the counter to hold my hand, I don't draw it away.

"Sadie, I told you before that we'd take things at your speed, and I meant it. Nothing has changed. I'm in this for the long haul with you, not just this week. All I ask is that you please don't pull away from me again. I'd like to keep building this with you, and it felt like you were finally starting to open up to me again."

My heart melts a little at his words, and I feel foolish for being so worried earlier. He's never pushed me, and always been a gentleman. "Thank you, Patrick. I feel the same way. I guess I got overwhelmed when those stupid alarms went off, and my brain started racing a mile a minute. I know what they're expecting, and Faith already warned me not to put it off because we could get sent to some sort of 'intensive getaway'"—I use finger quotes—"which is basically solitary confinement for couples."

His eyebrows shoot up in surprise. "Are you serious?"

I nod. "I would not joke about that."

He runs a hand through his dark hair, and I can't tell if it's with annoyance or anger. "Don't worry about that, okay? I will go and talk with the director if I need to. They're going to have to give us some time here, and it doesn't matter where they send us, that is not changing." His voice takes on a protective undertone, and a little shiver runs down my back when he squeezes my fingers.

I stare into his deep blue eyes, and once again I find myself thankful that he's who I'm doing this with. *Were it not for the political issues, he'd fit right into my family.* I frown, realizing we need to discuss his family's political expectations, too.

"Patrick, I know we won't be meeting each other's families for a while, but what are your parents expecting, exactly?"

He runs his hand through his hair again, and this time I can tell he's agitated by my question. He lets out a tired sigh before answering, "That is an excellent question, Sadie."

The oven timer beeps, saving him for a moment from answering. I slide the tray out of the oven with the blue paisley oven mitt and set another timer for them to cool before turning back to him.

"Those smell amazing. Did you really make those from memory?" He sniffs the air like a cartoon character.

"Yeah, they're one of my favorites. I know the recipe by heart. Also, you told me once that your mom used to make you chocolate chip cookies, and I never did get around to making you any." I shrug one shoulder. "I'm a stress baker."

"I hate to say it, but I think you should be stressed more often if this is how you deal with it. Can I have one?"

I can't help but laugh at that; his excitement is endearing. "Sorry, you've got to wait for them to cool or else they'll fall apart. Besides, we're supposed to be talking about your family expectations, remember? You can't do that with a mouth full of cookies."

He groans. "That's the worst reason ever to not give me a cookie."

I shake my head and grab two small dessert plates out of the cabinet, and two short glasses. Surprise, they are all blue, too. Grabbing the milk carton from the fridge door, I fill the cups before nailing him with a no-nonsense look. "No talking—no cookies."

He raises both hands and says, "Okay, okay. To be honest, I think they're expecting me to come home soon and start running for office."

My jaw drops. I appreciate his honesty, but that's not what I expected him to say. "But, you've been living under an assumed name for years, and it sounds like you barely see them. Why would they expect you to come home and follow along in your dad's footsteps?"

He sinks his head into his hands. "As much as I'd like to *not* think about it, my parents think it's very likely that there'll be a vote to move the North American Alliance to a monarchy soon."

My stomach clenches at his admission. "Soon, like how soon?" I ask, even though I'm afraid to hear the answer.

"Within the next five years. The last time I spoke with my father, he said people would be much more comfortable if I was already involved in a public political position before that happens, so they can get to know me." I can still hear him, despite the fact that he's currently speaking the words to his feet.

I just stare at him, not sure what else to even ask. The timer beeps, and I woodenly put two warm, melty cookies onto each plate. Sliding one across to him, I dunk my cookie and take a bite. *Perfection. At least some things never change.*

He looks up, picks up the bigger cookie, and takes a huge bite. "Oh, my God. I will deny it if you ever try to tell her, but these are even better than my mom's." He shoves some errant crumbs in from the corner of his mouth. "If we weren't already married, I'd marry you again just for these cookies."

His enjoyment thaws my frozen thoughts, and I laugh. "You are actually not the first person to say something like that to me."

He finishes the cookie in his second bite. "Yeah, but I'm the one that got you, nonetheless." He closes his eyes happily as he chews and then takes a sip of his milk.

"And here I thought it was my uterus you were after," I joke, and he nearly snorts milk out his nose.

For the next two days, we spent long hours walking on the beach together, sometimes talking, sometimes simply holding hands and taking in the ocean. We also found a hidden stash of board games, which we played on the bed—because the TV was still flashing bubblegum pink. Each night they bring a catered dinner—which, yes, I was originally mad about, but has been delicious. The first night they brought us prime rib, mashed potatoes, and an assortment of veggies in a balsamic reduction. Last night was a whole roasted duck with delicious Asian-themed sides.

I can't wait to see what they bring us for dinner tonight. "Personally, I'm hoping for Italian," I say amiably as we walk back up the beach to our cottage.

"Italian? It's Okay, I guess, but I want barbecue." Patrick says it wistfully. "We haven't had barbecue once since we've been here."

"I don't think that's likely. It's been fancy food, not down-home cooking."

"I know, I'm just saying, would it kill them to give us some good ribs and garlic bread? No, it would not."

I chuckle at his valiant defense of barbecue as we walk up the steps. "Maybe there's a comment card you can send to the kitchen." I pat him on the back.

"That's a good idea. I'll ask the delivery guy when he gets here—which should be any minute." He rubs his palms together in anticipation, but my attention has been captured once again by our blinking TV.

"That can't be good," I say and elbow Patrick to get his attention, pointing to the new message flashing in gold script.

"Your presence is requested in the guest house at your earliest convenience," he reads off. "That's interesting. I wonder why they'd pull us out of our little cocoon?"

My heart sinks to my gut. "I bet we're going to get lectured on our lack of tracking . . ." I trail off.

"Well, if so, we'll set them straight." He wraps an arm around my shoulders and pulls me in for a quick peck. "Don't worry about it, Sadie. They can't rush us, even if they try."

I give him a small return smile, but my stomach is rolling in nervous anticipation. We turn and head right back out of the cottage, and make the short walk to the guest house. I hold Patrick's hand, and try not to think about the million ways this could be a bad thing.

We walk in the back door and are surprised to see a small crowd gathered in the sitting area. As soon as we walk in, Jared spots us and clinks on the side of a champagne flute with a butter knife.

"Now that we're all here, if I could get everyone's attention please! We have an exciting announcement," he says, enthusiasm clear in his tone.

Relief floods my system as a pink-shirted employee presses a champagne flute into my hand. Although, on closer inspection, it doesn't appear to be champagne in the glass.

"Today, we have a confirmed pregnancy!" Jared announces with a flourish, teeth glinting in a wide smile. "If you'd all raise your sparkling cider in a toast to the new parents, Teddy and Faith!" Cheers erupt around the room from the other couples and the staff, but my jaw hits the floor. I hurriedly scan the room, and spot Teddy and Faith standing towards the front of · the group. He's beaming down at her, and she looks happy but shocked.

"Can you believe it? Already?" Patrick looks down at me and takes in my shock. "Hey, this is good news!" He rubs my arm affectionately.

"I know, I'm really happy for them. I just can't believe they didn't tell us first," I stammer, still turning the news over in my mind. *They weren't kidding about a ninety-nine percent match.*

One by one, couples and staff alike come forward and offer congratulations and hugs to the parents-to-be. Patrick steers me to the back of the line, and my feet move without thought. *Teddy is going to be a father! I'm going to be an aunt again!* We continue shuffling forward, and eventually it's our turn. Faith sees me and her eyes start to water. Lips trembling, she throws her arms around me in a bruising hug.

"Sadie, it actually happened, can you believe it?" Her voice cracks on the last word, and a choked sob is all that comes out next. I squeeze her back tightly, and look at Teddy over her shoulder. He's patting Patrick on the back in that man-thumping way dudes do to avoid hugging. After a solid minute, Faith pulls back and puts both hands to her mouth, still in shock.

"Congratulations, Faith, I'm so happy for you," I say with sincerity. "For both of you," I add. Teddy pulls me in for a bear hug, and lifts my feet clean off the floor in the process.

"You'll be next, baby sister, and then our kids will grow up best friends," he whispers in my ear, and my eyes start to water. He puts me down, and I punch him in the arm.

"Don't make me cry, you idiot!" I hastily wipe at my eyes, willing the tears to go away before they start. "I can't believe you two didn't tell us!" I give him an accusing glare.

"We didn't know!" Faith cuts in. "Every day they collect a urine sample to test, and then your results load to your device later that evening. We weren't due for results for another hour." She looks up at Teddy, and gratefulness washes over her features. "Teddy, I can't tell you how much this means to me, after so long. I—" Her voice cuts off, and she's crying again.

This time it's Faith he wraps in a gentle bear hug. "I know, Faith. I know," he says soothingly.

Jared taps his fluted glass again to cut through the din of conversations around the room. "In celebration of this new life, we'll be throwing a banquet this evening for the entire property! Dinner will be served in half an hour, so feel free to mingle until then." He turns to Melissa, who's been at his side, beaming throughout his announcement. They have a short but intense conversation before breaking apart.

Melissa scans the room, and her determined look lands on us. She makes her way through the crowded room like a bullet. "Hey, you two, I need an appointment with you at the medical facility. How does tomorrow around 9:30 sound?" Her voice is syrupy sweet, with a no-nonsense undertone.

Patrick cuts right to the chase. "What is this about?"

"Let's not interrupt the celebration. I'll see you both promptly at 9:30." She turns and walks away without further room for argument.

I look at Patrick, worried. There's no way that's good.

SIX

THE PRINCIPAL'S OFFICE

The celebratory dinner passes in a blur. Faith looks like she's walking on a cloud, and Teddy looks elated the whole time. My heart clenches again, but this time with happiness. Faith deserves this. *Not that anyone else doesn't.* I think of all the girls we left behind at the NLC. I have to put them out of mind for now, as this celebration is all about Teddy and Faith, and the new little life she's growing. We sit directly across from them at dinner, and family-style trays of entrees, brought out in waves, cover the table in front of us at all times. The mood overall is jovial, and it's easy to pretend that the other shoe isn't going to drop tomorrow morning.

The wait staff keeps the sparkling cider flowing all evening, and before we know it, the dessert plates are empty and it's time to walk back to our cottages. Faith and I link arms for the long walk down the beach, and she presses her other hand gently against her lower abdomen.

"I can't believe there's a baby in there, after all this time," she says softly. "I don't feel any different. Shouldn't I feel different?" She looks at me, concern etched into her lovely moonlit features.

"I don't know for sure, but I think that part comes later. I'm sure you can talk to the medical director about what to expect."

She nods, appeased for now. "Just think, Sadie. You'll probably be right behind us in a month or two! Isn't it exciting to imagine our kids growing up together? They'll each have a built-in best friend. I would have killed for that when I was growing up."

My stomach rolls at the idea of being pregnant in a month. Or two months. I know it's likely, assuming Patrick and I are ready to take our physical relationship to the next level soon. But, a baby? A living, breathing human to take care of? *I'm not ready.*

Thankfully we arrive at their cabin, and Teddy steals Faith from my arm to lead her up to their front door. She throws one last wave over her shoulder at me, before leaning her head on his shoulder as he unlocks their front door.

Teddy is going to be a great father. Sure, he's a major goofball, and he's still young. But he's got a loyal streak a mile wide, and he's already fallen hook, line, and sinker for Faith. I can't imagine their baby will be any different.

"Penny for your thoughts?" Patrick says as we make our way down the last stretch of beach to the next cabin, ours.

I shake my head, unsure where to begin. Staring out at the moonlight reflected over the crashing waves, it feels like I could will it all away—the expectations, the oversight. Will away the forced urgency on our relationship. But, our relationship . . . I wouldn't wish that away. The lies and the distance between us, yes. But him? The man at my side? No. He's already burrowed into the very center of my soul, and I know deep down that I've been forever changed by even our brief time together.

We make our way up the front steps, and he lets me keep my thoughts to myself. With a small smile, he goes to the hall bathroom and I hear the rush of the shower turning on, the start of his nightly routine. It's funny how I know that small detail about him already, even though we haven't been living together long. And yet, it's impossible for me to not know that he's a morning person who loves the thrill of running before the sun's up. He's permanently kind and treats everyone he meets well, despite who his father is; despite who he might be. But also, he really, *really* sucks at playing Scrabble. The corner of my mouth quirks up as I remember yesterday when I'd discovered that tidbit. I'd crushed him, but he took it with grace.

The fact is, the longer we live together, the more I find myself drawn to him, like a moth drawn to a flame. The only question is, am I going to end up burnt up and destroyed, just like one of those moths? He's lied to me once; how can I trust that he won't again? And can I trust him beyond friendship, with a real marriage, and everything that comes with that?

The shower door claps shut down the hall, and I realize then that I've been standing, frozen in the doorway with my own thoughts. I force my feet to move, and go draw a bath in the other bathroom. One day at a time.

It takes me forever to fall asleep, and then it's a restless night of tossing and turning, in and out of the covers. Finally I drift off, and when I wake, I grow slowly aware of a warm and firm shoulder under my cheek and hands.

With a blink, I take a deep breath and the scent of Patrick floods my nose. Stiffening, it hits me. I am wrapped around Patrick's chest like a barnacle, and his firm bicep is under my head. His breathing is steady and deep, so I slowly start to extract myself in hopes that he won't wake up and realize I'd cuddled up against him like a lost puppy in the night.

Before I make it three inches away, he rumbles, "Good morning. Did you finally get some sleep?"

I jump to a sitting position, and the cold air of our room smacks all the parts of me that were so warm pressed against him.

This is so awkward! "Yes, uhm, how about you?" I push the bird's nest of my hair away from my face, but the determined chestnut strands are still visible from the corner of my eye. I look anywhere but at his face. My eyes land on his chest, where his sleep shirt is pushed partway up and revealing a flat, toned stomach. Quickly I dart them elsewhere, where they land back on his face and his cheesy grin.

"Just fine, thanks. You don't have to be embarrassed, Sadie. We're married. If you want to cuddle, it's allowed." He lazily sits up and leans in close to me, where I feel like I've been rooted to the spot by his magnetism. "Encouraged, even," he says in a whisper before pressing a warm, languid kiss to the side of my neck and climbing out of bed.

I shamelessly watch as he pads off to the bathroom, but he catches me when he stops to give me a wink before leaving the room. After a moment, when my heart climbs back down my throat to where it belongs, I scurry out of bed and into the bathroom, shutting the door a little too hard behind me. I spin and stare in the large mirror over the sink at my wild eyes and messy mop of hair. *What is he trying to do to me?!*

I finish my morning routine as slowly as possible, but finally I can't hide any longer or we'll be late for our meeting with the medical director. *Ugh, Melissa.* She's acted so sunny and shiny until now, but something tells me that's about to change.

I exit the bathroom dressed in my favorite jeans, flannel, and boots to find a smiling Patrick sipping a cup of coffee. "You ready?"

With a nod, he offers me a hand, and we head to the medical facility.

The tall glass doors open automatically, and warm air filled with a disinfectant tang rushes out and slaps us in the face. I wrinkle my nose at the sharp odor, but quickly put my shoulders back and my game face on as I spot Melissa waiting by the desk. She's wearing pink scrubs again, but today her shoes have winged unicorns.

I am not scared of anybody who is wearing those shoes, I tell myself as she greets us.

"Patrick, Sadie! So good to see you both this morning. If you'll follow me to my office, I have a few things I'd like to discuss with you." She smiles, but the hard set of her jaw belies her jovial words. She spins on her unicorn-adorned heel, and leads us down the hallway to a door we didn't see on our tour. She holds it for us to enter, and then closes it with a quiet click.

Taking seats in front of her desk, she crosses behind it and sits before clicking rapidly on a tablet. The lights dim, and her entire office wall to the left of us pops up a calendar display with bright pink highlights on it.

"So, it seems we have a small issue." She cuts right to the chase. "Today is the final day of your fertile week, and we do not have any tracking activity for you two. What's going on?" She clasps her hands under her chin and pins us to our seats with her stare.

We're both silent for a beat before Patrick speaks up. "We are taking our time to get to know each other a bit better before taking things to the next level. As you know from our file, our time at the NLC was not exactly restful. There was a kidnapping attempt, and Sadie had *seven* matches to contend with. Neither one of us wants to rush into this." His voice is calm, but his tone is no-nonsense.

My heart warms at his words, and the way he includes himself instead of blaming it on me being a chicken.

She taps her index fingers together thoughtfully, and it's a long moment before she responds. "I see."

It's silent for another beat, before she looks down and taps her tablet a few times and the lights go back up to normal.

"I understand that you two had a bumpier ride getting here than some couples, and I sympathize. I really do. *However*, the primary objective of this program is no secret. The human race is in trouble, and we can't let perfectly healthy couples wait around for the mood to strike. *Every* month is a critical opportunity, right from the start." She pauses, to see if her words are having any effect on us.

Patrick crosses his arms over his chest and stares her down.

Melissa is the first to look away, but she isn't dissuaded. "I have no desire to be the bad guy here, I do hope you know that. But I also have a responsibility to ensure that this program pushes every couple to their best chance of conception. And we simply cannot have you two squandering your time in this way. So, this is your only free pass. If you have not tracked anything before next month's fertile week begins, we'll have to assign you to an intensive getaway until that changes." She purses her lips and shifts her eyes between the two of us.

It's all I can do not to let my anger show, so I look down to my lap. Patrick on the other hand, feels no such hesitation. "Listen, Melissa. I understand you're in a tough spot. But Sadie is my wife. And I *refuse* to rush her before she's ready. So, you can send us on an intensive getaway. Hell, you can send us to Mars if you want. But you will. Not. Force. This. Not until *she's* ready. Do you understand?" He punctuates his anger with a fingertip to the top of her desk with each staccato syllable.

She leans back in her desk chair, but she doesn't look intimidated by his display of fury. Instead, she focuses her attention on me. "So, Sadie, are you having some anxiety about physical intimacy? Is that the issue here?" She waves between us, as if the problem will materialize for her to diagnose.

"No." I finally speak up with indignation. "I'm not having anxiety. I was just raised that you should get to know someone before you get physical with them. This program doesn't change the way I was raised, and I'm not a girl who's comfortable jumping into bed with someone I don't know well."

She shakes her head slowly. "Sadie, I'm disappointed. I thought you knew how important this program is for the future of humanity. There's so much more at stake here than your small-town ideals. I do hope you'll reconsider. Either way, you two can see yourselves out. I have another appointment." She picks up her tablet, and brushes past us out the door without another glance.

I turn to Patrick, unsure how to take the abrupt ending to this unpleasant meeting. He reaches over and wraps my hand in his, thumb gently grazing my knuckles and leaving a pleasant tingle in its wake.

"Don't worry about it, Sadie. They can't force us, even if they send us on an intensive getaway. Who cares? This is not up for them to decide, and all the threats in the world can't change what we decide. Okay?" He lifts his other hand and runs his thumb gently along my chin. "Do you mind if we run to the guest house before we head back? I'd like to run by the front desk and ask them if we have any letters."

I force a smile for his benefit, but I'm not so sure they won't try to force this, one way or another. One month. I let out a long breath. It's not a lot of time, but I guess it will have to be enough.

Patrick heads straight for the front desk, so I wander over to the dining room to see if they have any snacks set out this afternoon. To my surprise, Odette is already there, standing immobile in front of the side table which, to my delight, is covered in fresh baked goods.

"Hey, Odette." I greet her as I grab a large plate—I've got to have room to get some snacks for Patrick, too—but she doesn't respond. "Odette? You okay?" I ask, concerned with her seemingly catatonic state.

She startles as if jolted, and finally notices me standing next to her. "Oh, hello, Sadie. Am I in your way? I'll go." Her voice is flat, and she turns to leave with silent grace.

"Wait, don't go! You haven't even gotten a snack yet." I point to the well-laden table.

She raises one eyebrow in surprise. "You're right, I haven't." She gives me a tentative smile.

"What are you waiting for? Dig in!" I hand her my plate, and grab another. "So, no Dominic today?"

She stiffens at the mention of his name, but accepts the plate, and focuses on the pastries.

"Not right now—I needed some time to myself." Her voice is all cool control, just like the rest of her.

"That's hard to come by around here, but I understand. I used to spend a lot more time solo, at the ranch. Well, solo with Morgan, my horse," I say wistfully.

"Yes, it is very difficult to find a moment to think."

"I'm sorry to interrupt you. I'll get out of your hair and let you get back to it." My plate is already three-quarters full of flaky pastry goodness, while hers is still noticeably empty.

Odette lowers the plate, dropping all pretense. "Sadie, do you have feelings for Patrick?"

Her abrupt change of topic startles me. "Uhm, well . . . kind of? We're still working on that," I stammer, unsure what to say to her given the complexity of my relationship with Patrick right now.

She nods. "Well, Dominic isn't a bad man. But I don't love him, and he doesn't love me. He still loves Carla, even though she's married and already pregnant with another man's baby." Her eyes drift from the table down to her toes and, for the first time, I catch a glimpse of the pain underneath her icy façade.

"I'm sorry, Odette. That has to be incredibly difficult." I reach out, resting a hand on her forearm.

"It is. It is incredibly difficult. I—" She stops, unable to articulate her feelings.

"Would you like to talk about it? I won't share whatever you tell me. It can stay between us," I offer, but I sincerely doubt she'll take me up on it. *Although, if you'd asked me yesterday if I'd be having a personal chat with Odette at all, I'd have laughed at you.*

She's silent for a long moment. "No, no—I wouldn't want to detract from your day. I am sure you and Patrick are off to enjoy your honeymoon."

I snort. "Not quite. I've got time. Come on, let's go grab that table in the corner." I walk over, and plop the overflowing plate between us.

She follows, and perches daintily in the chair across from me.

"Don't be shy—what's your favorite?" I ask, gesturing to the plate between us.

Her eyebrows lift nearly to her hairline when she takes in the smorgasbord I've selected, but she selects a small custard tart dusted with powdered sugar without comment and sets it on her plate.

"So, tell me about you and Dominic. Are you two a good genetic match, at least? Are you friends, or trying to be?"

She tucks her head, and fiddles with the edge of the tart crust before answering, "Not terribly strong, no. Around sixty percent. And in the beginning, we tried to be friends. It isn't easy for me to open up to people." She glances up briefly at the admission before continuing to fiddle with the dessert.

"Well, that's all right. It takes time to build up trust in a relationship. Especially with obstacles to overcome." The last part is for me, as much as her.

Her mouth is set in a tight line, but she nods. "I thought we had a chance to at least get through this in a companionable way, if not as a true love match. But he's still pining for Carla, and I am not going to compete for affections that I know I can't win."

I reach across and cover her hand with mine. "Hey, there are no guarantees in this life, Odette. You two can still build a friendship, over time. Maybe don't focus on love first. Maybe you could try to speak openly with him about how you're feeling, and how it hurts to see him pining for another woman. I can't imagine him intentionally trying to hurt you. He is probably oblivious. He might not realize that it still hurts, even if you two aren't in love right now."

Patrick comes strolling into the dining room at that moment, clearly looking for me. I discreetly wave him off under the table, where Odette can't see me. He looks surprised at my table companion, but walks back out without her noticing.

"I don't know if I can, Sadie. He is a good man, but he wants nothing to do with me. How am I supposed to overlook that? How am I supposed to have a physical relationship with someone who I know wants someone else?"

The depth of her problem sinks in, and I feel awful for her. Patrick has his issues, sure. But at least I don't have to try to make it through this program while watching him pine for someone else, and knowing he's thinking of another woman. "I'm so sorry, Odette. What's the alternative? Is there anything you can do? I heard—" I pause, embarrassed that the source of my information is gossip. I clear my throat, and forge ahead. "I heard that you two have already been on an intensive getaway. Is there nothing else the program can offer to help you two work through this? You aren't the first ones to leave someone else behind."

"Well, I have an appointment with Melissa to discuss some things. It's not possible to separate before the three years are up, but, they might be willing to help remove the *personal* element from the process." She breaks a single crumb off her pastry, and tastes it.

It takes me a minute to realize what she's alluding to. "Oh, they're going to do a fertility treatment for you? That's pretty invasive, isn't it?"

She shrugs one shoulder delicately. "Not as invasive as the alternative."

I can't contain my snort. "Sorry, I'm not laughing at you. You're right, I've just never heard it put in quite those terms before."

She looks up again and a smile is playing at the corner of her lips. My heart warms at her willingness to open up to me.

"Well, I really hope they'll help you, if that is what you'd prefer. And I want you to know, you're not the only couple here with problems. Patrick and I are working on things, too. It's not all glitter and rainbows for us."

The concern on her face is genuine, and I find myself questioning all of my original assumptions about her. "I am sorry to hear that. I hope you two are able to come together and work through it. Is there anything you would like to discuss? I will keep your confidence, as you'll keep mine."

I swallow, and suddenly I'm the one staring at my plate, the pastry I'd been enjoying before turning dry in my mouth. "I fell for him, hook line and sinker. And I picked him, out of my other options. Sent other really nice men home, because I was so sure he was it." I pause, and force myself to meet her eyes. I have nothing to be ashamed of here. "But then, after the wedding, I found out he'd been dishonest with me. It shook me, and it shook my faith in him. My faith in my ability to choose a trustworthy person."

She shakes her head, her expression grim. "That is hard to recover from. Has he been honest with you since then?"

"I think so. But, it's hard to trust again. It's hard to pick myself back up, trust myself to know who I can believe anymore." A lump forms in my throat. "What if he lies again? What if there's more he hasn't told me?"

She taps a slim finger on the table, thinking about what I've confessed. "Did he tell you himself?"

"Sort of? He was caught out, and then fessed up."

"Hmm, it's a toss-up, then. Liars will always lie. But an honest man will make it right. The question is, which is Patrick? I'm sure you'll figure it out. Actions don't lie, even if handsome men do." She shakes her head, "Well, I should get back, and I'm sure you should, as well. Thank you for talking with me, Sadie. I don't have any friends here, and it means a lot that you were willing to listen."

"You're wrong, Odette. You have a friend here now—me." I give her a warm smile, meaning every word.

Her return smile is timid, but it's a start. She takes the plate with her single pastry, and heads out of the dining room. I follow behind her, and find Patrick waiting on a tufted bench in the hallway.

"Everything good?" he asks, as he stands and we walk towards the back door.

"Yeah, actually it is."

"Want to talk about it?" He reaches over and twines his fingers with mine, and the simple contact melts my heart.

"Nah, it's girl stuff," I say lightly.

"Okay. Are some of those for me?" He sounds hopeful, so I pass him the plate.

"Go nuts. But the cheese Danishes are mine," I warn.

SEVEN
UNREST

Patrick and I spend the rest of the day in our cottage, playing board games and reading, as has become our routine. We don't discuss the meeting further, even though it hangs in the air between us like a heavy curtain. Our living room is still filled with unpleasant blinking pink light, so we spend the majority of the day in our room, lounging on the bed.

Finally, the knock comes on our door that signals our dinner's delivery. Patrick meets the delivery man, and I hear them exchange a few muffled words as I make my way to the kitchen. We've taken to eating our fancy dinners at the island bar stools, so I wait there as he brings in the tray and sets it down. I notice immediately, however, that there aren't just silver cloche domes on the tray tonight, as there were the last few nights. There is a baby pink box tied with a matching ribbon nestled at the center of the tray.

"What's that?" I ask Patrick, pointing to the small box.

He frowns. "I was told it's for you. They didn't tell me what's in it, only that Melissa sent it."

That can't be good. I pick up the box as he starts removing the shiny silver cloches from the food, revealing platters piled high with ribs, greens, and mac and cheese. The final dome hides a basket of pillowy-looking yeast rolls and mounds of whipped butter. I stare, momentarily distracted from the box I'd yet to open.

"Did you seriously track down the chef? This is nothing like the food they've been sending us, but it smells amazing!" I reach for a roll and take a small nibble of the corner before setting it down and returning my attention to the box.

"I didn't track down anyone in the kitchen, although I was discussing the lack of barbecue with Teddy last night at dinner. I guess one of the staff overheard our conversation." His frown deepens, despite the delicious spread in front of us.

I reach out a hand for his and twine my fingers between his larger ones. "Hey, I'm sure they were just trying to be accommodating. The staff here seem very eager to please."

He meets my eyes briefly and nods before turning to grab blue plates from the cabinets. "I'm sure you're right, it's just disconcerting to think someone was eavesdropping on our conversation." He turns back around with plates and starts filling them. "Are you going to open that thing, or use it as a paperweight?"

I sigh, and tug on the ribbon. It falls away easily, and I lift the lid from the small box. Inside is a folded piece of paper. When I open it, feminine script fills the small page.

Sadie, there is no reason to let anxiety stop you from doing your duty to society. Take these with dinner, and let Patrick do the rest.

—Melissa

My jaw hits the floor as I set the note aside, and nestled into a bit of jewelry padding is not, in fact, a gift, but two small purple pills. My hands start to shake as fury rolls over me from my head to my toes. I grip the box so tightly in my hand that the corners start to crumple in on themselves.

Looking up from the plates he set in front of our usual seats, Patrick asks, "What's in the box?"

I wordlessly shove the note at him, and walk over to the kitchen sink. I turn the water on full blast, and then start the garbage disposal with a flick of one finger.

Patrick reads quickly and says, "You've got to be kidding me. What's in that box, Sadie?"

I hold up the box, showing him the two purple pills nestled inside. Before he can comment, I pick them up and drop them, one after the other, right into the angry maw of the garbage disposal. The grinding sound rings hollow in my pounding ears. I flip off the disposal after it's returned to its normal hum, and brace both hands on the countertop.

"This is ridiculous. They can't seriously prefer you to drug yourself than to wait a month or two. How is that supposed to be keeping you in good health, exactly?" His rant falls on deaf ears, and my vision grows tunneled as I just stare into the stream of water flowing out of the shiny faucet. My knuckles are white on the countertop.

I feel like screaming or hitting something. But the people who deserve it aren't here, and the message is clear. *Get in line, or we'll put you in line.*

Arms gently encircle my waist from behind, and my mind slowly focuses back on the present moment. I pry one hand free from my death grip on the countertop and lower it to Patrick's where it rests softly on my waist.

"I can't do this. I can't live like this, Patrick. I'm not some zoo animal that can live under a microscope!" My breaths are coming in fast gulps now, and for the first time, I feel truly panicked. My rage is still there, burning in my gut. But without an outlet, the panic has surged to the forefront.

"Hey, hey—it's going to be okay. It's not okay. Not really, but it will be." He strokes my hair gently with his free hand, and I close my eyes and lean into his touch. Eventually I turn in his arms and sink into his hard chest. My sobs break free and it's like a dam bursting after all this time, anger and frustration pouring out in the only way available to me.

"We can't let them get away with this, Patrick. They don't deserve this kind of power over people's lives," I say it quietly, but I know he hears me when his chin bobs against the top of my head.

"I know, Sadie. I know."

The next morning, our blinking pink television has returned to normal, thank God. We meander out and down to the guest house to have breakfast and see what everyone else is up to today.

Once we arrive in the dining room, we spot Teddy and Faith sitting at a large table with Emmett and Carolina, so we walk over to join them.

"Hey, newlyweds! Nice of you to join us." Emmett is the first to greet us, grinning widely. He seems to always be welcoming, which I appreciate.

"Good morning," Patrick greets him in return as we grab two empty seats.

A pink-shirted waiter hurries over with a basket of their signature pastries, and takes our breakfast order. Once that's taken care of, we turn our attention to the other couples at the table.

"What are you guys all doing today?" I ask.

"We've got appointments at the medical facility all morning for early screenings," Faith says, her voice betraying her nerves.

"I think we're going to stay in and watch a movie. We hiked out to the lighthouse yesterday, so we're pretty beat," Carolina says. "You guys are welcome to join us, if you'd like! We haven't had a lot of company since we've been here," she says with sadness.

"Odette and Dominic not much for group activities?" Teddy asks.

She shakes her head. "No, Dominic seems like a nice guy, but Odette barely talks. We've been trying to let them have their space, but it doesn't seem to have improved any."

I see an opportunity, and I take it. "Have there been any other couples here, or just you two so far?"

"There was another couple when we first got here, Katie and Liam, but they got pregnant and had some issues, so had to transfer over to York for a procedure." She realizes what she said, and darts her eyes over to Faith's anxious face. "I'm pretty sure it was something minor, nothing life threatening," she adds with a forced smile.

Faith gazes down at her barely-touched plate with a troubled expression. "It's okay, Carolina, this is my third match. I've seen couples get sent to the Reproductive Issues Department plenty of times."

Carolina looks relieved. "I'm sure you have. I've always thought they should have named it something better. I mean, 'RID' is kind of ominous, don't you think?" she muses as she takes a bite of her omelet.

Faith looks up with a small smile. "Yeah, I thought the same thing. Not that any of the names are great. I mean, this place is beautiful, but Mairmont Honeymoon Resort is a pretty bland name."

I snort. "Any chance to remind us why we're here—I expected something more along the lines of 'Baby Factory.' The NLC wasn't any better. Remember the dorms? Instead of calling it a dorm, they had to call it the 'Future Mothers' Wing" on the plaque by the front door."

Our pleasant chat is interrupted by one of the staff rushing in and turning on one of the televisions behind the waiters' service area. The screen pops on, and he urgently selects a news channel. The volume is low from this distance, but the message is clear enough.

A blonde reporter in her late forties is giving the report at a desk, with live footage of men holding signs outside of the capitol building in Wrightsville. "Just this morning, I've heard news that a vote has been called once again about changing the political structure of our nation. Unlike last time, the bill is said to have near-unanimous support, and comes on the tail of the major leak earlier this week that the prime minister's son has in fact been married as part of the Compulsory Marriage Program. We have no official news that the two events are related, but it seems likely at this time."

I can feel the color drain from my face, and I look over to see Patrick—also pulled from his conversation by the sudden intrusion—looking grim.

Emmett is the first to comment. "Poor bastard. You know he tries hard to stay out of the limelight since nobody knows what he looks like, but vultures are everywhere. Do you think they'll really turn the North American Alliance into a monarchy, though? Marriage is great and all, but that's no guarantee he's going to be able to continue the line, not yet."

Teddy speaks up, giving Patrick another moment to compose himself. "It does seem premature, but I'm sure there's more to the story than we know. They've been bandying the idea around for years, even before the son was married off. This is heaping fuel onto the fire that was already burning. I'm sure if it passes, he'll keep getting assigned a new wife until one produces an heir."

My stomach flips, turning against the cheese Danish I'd already scarfed down. The thought of Patrick re-married to someone else sends a wave of heat over me. *Am I really jealous? I don't want to be a political figure. I want to go back home to the ranch as soon as I can. And if Patrick and I stay together, that probably won't be an option. But the idea of divorcing him—* I shudder. Deep down, I'm already attached. The idea of going home a divorcee, for no reason other than his job, doesn't sit well with me. I can already see the looks of disappointment etched into my parents' faces if I were to go home and tell them that. It's not an option.

Hey, Mom, yeah, that's right. I was married to a really nice, gorgeous, understanding guy. Yep, we had two kids together, and then I kicked him to the curb because I didn't want the hassle of being a political wife. Or queen. Or, whatever. The thought trails off, and I'm pulled back into the present by Faith's question.

"What do you think, Sadie? Do you think it matters if we're a monarchy? I don't really see how it matters one way or another. We haven't elected a new prime minister in over a decade, anyway."

I blink twice, trying to think of something intelligent to say. "Well, it's definitely a huge political difference, but with the way things are for women already, I don't know how much of a difference it makes to us individually. We already can't hold jobs or get a higher education until we've had children, and raising kids makes it harder to pursue a career, regardless of who's in charge. Plus, with the latest emergency declaration, I'm not sure how that would work even after we have kids, since there's no longer a cap of two babies and you're released." I frown, remembering Jenna and how much she wanted to go join the NAA ranks and become a pilot.

"Well, it's impossible to tell without knowing the son. I mean, he could be like his dad and keep the status quo, or he could be better or worse for women's rights," Carolina muses. "I'm sure he's not going to do away with the program either way though, with the population numbers still so bad."

"Can you imagine how his new wife must feel? It's a pure stroke of luck to have the right genes to snag a could-be-prince," Faith says dreamily.

I stay silent, as it doesn't feel lucky to me that Patrick could become a prince. In fact, I'm rooting for it not to happen. As long as we're still a democracy, he can live the life he wants, not be forced into a political role. That's one way in which it's as much out of his hands as it is mine. He would be swept up in a role he couldn't escape, too. A pang of compassion strikes my heart, and I reach for Patrick's hand under the table and I give it a small squeeze. He squeezes my hand in return, and my heart warms.

The employee with the remote turns up the volume, and the reporter's words wash over us again. "I'd like to draw your attention to the protestors we have outside the capitol. Rather than protesting the monarchy, you'll see that most are actually in favor. However, we are seeing several signs calling for an unveiling of the prime minister's son. Historically speaking, the people would know who the monarchy would be passed on to from birth of the child, but our situation is different given the fact that we don't currently have a royal family in place. While the public has no way of forcing the issue, his extreme seclusion from the public eye up until now could negatively impact the vote's outcome."

The screen fills with the feed of men outside the capitol holding signs with crowns painted on them and sayings like "Monarchy Now," and it flashes to one that says "Prince Royce,

You're Our Choice." I feel Patrick stiffen beside me, and he squeezes my hand again.

The blonde news anchor pops back into the frame. "As you can see, the question on everyone's mind right now is, who is the mysterious son of Prime Minister Royce, and who is his new bride? As a nation, it seems that everyone wants to know that our political foundation is secure, as well as our future. I'm Candy Thomas, and we at NAA One are always first to bring you global news."

"What's crazy is, this guy is out there at a honeymoon resort right now, same as us. How do you think they are still keeping his identity a secret? He's got to have a security detail, right?" Teddy postulates.

Patrick finally speaks, "Maybe, maybe not. The security at the NLC and each of the resorts is top notch anyway. You saw that there was a kidnapping attempt in Georada, so the stakes are already high as long as there are extremists trying to abduct women."

Teddy claps him on the shoulder. "Patrick was a guard at the Georada NLC before getting matched with Sadie, so he would know."

Chimes start coming from Faith's mini-tablet, which she pulls out of a pocket. "Ten minutes until our appointment. Are you done, Teddy? We can start walking over so we don't have to rush."

"Sure thing, beautiful." He slides his chair out and gives me a quick peck on the cheek before taking her hand. "See y'all later. We'll try to swing by for a movie tonight when we're done with our tests."

We all wave as they leave, but before they're out the door my mind is already turning over the implications of the growing unrest.

After making plans to meet up for an evening movie, we excuse ourselves from breakfast and head back to our cottage. The silence between us is tense, like a rubber band about to snap. An outsider would probably not notice anything, but I can see that Patrick's jaw is clenched and his stride is choppier than usual. His agitation is clear to me, but I am not sure how to help him.

He opens our front door with robotic movements, and holds it for me to enter. Rather than slam it, he shuts it with a quiet click. I fidget with the hem of my jacket as I wait for him to start the conversation.

He starts pacing between the living room and dining room table without a word. He runs his hands through his hair twice and makes about ten laps before he starts speaking, "I can't figure out who would have leaked the information that I got married. It seems like a targeted thing, meant to stir up another monarchy vote, well before it would have come up again otherwise. The last two times someone called for a vote, they were nearly seven years apart. It hasn't even been three years since the last vote was called!"

He throws his hands in the air, and I mentally turn over what he's said. "Can you contact your parents and ask if they know who leaked the information? It can't be widely known, right?"

"No, it is a very small circle of people who know my current identity—that's what's bothering me. Although, given they leaked only the marriage and not my assumed name, I would guess that they are outside that circle, and perhaps heard the vague information inside my father's office. It's very possible he, or Mom, confided in someone about the marriage, and someone overheard." His lips press together in an angry line. "Unfortunately, I can't contact them without potentially giving the leak my name and location—until it's determined who the informant was. I imagine they would have already contacted me to give me a heads up if they'd already identified the person."

"So, we're stuck waiting for them to reach out, then?"

He nods once, sharply but doesn't stop pacing.

"Hey, come here." I hold out my arms, and he stops and takes the two steps to reach me. I slowly slide my hands up to his shoulders, and wrap them softly around the back of his neck.

His intense gaze turns questioning as I play with the hair under my fingertips. "I'm sorry someone told the press about our wedding, and I'm sorry that it's caused the monarchy bill to come back to a vote sooner than you were expecting—" I trail off, but continue rubbing small soothing circles on the back of his neck.

His eyes flutter closed, and he touches his forehead to mine. "It's not the first time the media has gotten hold of information about me, but this one could have a serious impact. It's not only my privacy at stake anymore. It's the future governance of an entire *continent of people*."

The weight of those words sink in, but I don't stop rubbing. Instead, I up the ante with a tender kiss to his cheek. "There's nothing we can do about that right now, Patrick. As much as I'd like to wave a magic wand and make all of it disappear, you can't change who you are, any more than I can change who I am."

He wraps his arms around me and squeezes me tightly. We stay like that for a long moment, not speaking, simply soaking in the comfort of each other's arms. It feels so right to be here with him, comforting him.

"Thank you, Sadie. You're right, there's nothing to be done but wait for now. It's unusual for my parents to let something like this get out. They've kept me out of the spotlight for so long, it doesn't make sense to me that they would suddenly slip up after all these years. I hate that my name and family could be putting you in danger." The words come out slightly muffled against my hair.

I pull back and look him in the eye, so there's no mistaking my sincerity. "Patrick, I was in danger before I picked you. Being a polymorph, heck, being a fertile woman at all in this society puts a kidnapping target on my back. That's not your fault, and right now no one except us and the director back in Georada knows I'm your wife."

He sighs. "I still don't like it. If something happened to you because of your connection to me, I'd never forgive myself. I—" He stops, and it seems like he's going to say something else, but he doesn't. He swallows once, hard and looks down at our feet. "I'm sorry to put you through this."

I squeeze both of his hands. "It's okay, Patrick. It really is. We're going to be fine. What do you say I bake some more cookies to take over to Carolina and Emmett's place for the movie tonight?"

His eyes are still sad, but he smiles at me anyway. "That sounds good. Chocolate chip?"

I pour all of my enthusiasm into my return smile. "Anything you want. But you're doing the dishes."

He barks out a startled laugh, but trails behind me into the kitchen without complaint.

EIGHT

RUN FOR COVER

The next day dawns, and I find myself once again wrapped around Patrick's warm torso like an octopus. This time, I've even tossed my left leg over him to stop his escape. A small part of me wonders if I should feel guilty that I've blocked him from getting up for his beloved early morning run again, but I dismiss the idea. If he wanted to get up early like usual, he could still sneak out.

Before I even move, he teases me. "Good morning, sleeping beauty. Did you sleep well?"

My blush spreads like wildfire as I withdraw my leg. "Yes, I did. How about you? No run this morning?"

His chest rumbles under my cheek with a low laugh. "Somehow I couldn't disentangle myself and face the cold."

"I thought you liked the early morning cold?"

He wraps both arms around me, and gives me a quick kiss on the top of the head. "Given the choice between running alone in the cold, and staying in bed and snuggling with my gorgeous, warm wife—it's no contest."

His words send a thrill of warmth tingling through me. I smack a quick kiss on his chest before answering, "You're not so bad to snuggle, yourself. Although you are kind of lumpy." I poke his hard pectoral muscle with my finger.

This time his laugh is deep, and before I even realize what's happening, I'm on my back, staring up at a grinning Patrick. "In a poking mood this morning, are we? Well, I guess I've got to poke these ribs then!" His fingers walk up the side of my ribcage, and it sends a jolt of lighting straight through my thin sleep shirt. For a moment I'm frozen in surprise, but then the wave of ticklishness pulls me under.

"Patrick! You have to stop! Oh, my gosh, I'm going to pee!" I smack his hands away from my ribs, but his grin turns devilish and he continues the attack.

I flip to my stomach to protect my ribs from his questing fingertips, and he trails both hands down my back in a slow maneuver instead. I freeze, every muscle clenched in anticipation of the next wave of tickling, but it doesn't come. His warm hands span nearly my entire back, and this time when I shudder, it's from heat, not ticklishness. He slowly works his hands up and down a few times, and it feels like my bones are melting from the sensation. A single sigh escapes me, and he presses a warm kiss at the base of my neck.

In that instant, two things happened—first, it felt like his kiss sent a wave of molten heat through me. Second, it felt like my entire body locked up on instinct. Patrick felt me stiffen underneath his attentive hands, and sat back on his heels. "Are you okay, Sadie?"

"Yes, I'm fine, totally fine. Just, uhm, ready to get going and grab some breakfast. I'm starving!" I practically leap from the bed and the bathroom door slips from my clumsy fingers and slams shut behind me much harder than I meant it to. Rather than race to get ready as I'd told Patrick, I give myself a long look in the bathroom mirror. *When am I going to stop being a chicken? I'm falling for him. More than falling for him.*

I hear the sound of Patrick's footsteps retreating to the hall, and the soft click of the other bathroom door closing behind him. Only then do I blow out a heavy sigh and give myself one last shake of my head in the mirror. *If I can't even admit how I feel to myself, how will I admit it to him? And what happens once we take the next step?*

My body methodically moves through my morning routine, but my mind won't stop replaying this morning's interactions over again with Patrick. It's the elephant in the room, the building question of when we'll take things to the next step. But, he's made it clear many times over that the decision is fully in my hands. What if I can't make the leap? Will we be stuck hanging in this in-between zone forever? No, *because the resort won't let us wait around forever.*

After I'm dressed, I make my way out to the living room where Patrick's sipping a cup of coffee on the couch. My breath catches at his attractiveness. He's wearing simple jeans and a long-sleeved blue Henley which makes the blue of his eyes shine brightly. So casual, yet so irresistible to me. I stand there, uncertain, and the silence grows between us like a balloon about to burst. He seems unbothered, but it's like an itch to my skin that I have to scratch.

"I'm sorry I froze up before, I—I have no idea how to go from where we are now to where . . ." I trail off, unable to vocalize what was eating me up inside, despite my best efforts. Frustration rolls over me in a wave. *Why is this so hard for me?*

He balances the coffee cup on his knee. "Sadie, you don't have to apologize to me. It's okay, we're taking things slow. Things will progress in their own way. I'm happy with whatever is making you happy." He frowns slightly. "Unless, it's not making you happy? Do you feel like things are moving too fast, still?"

I groan. "No, that's the thing. They're not too fast. Maybe—" I swallow past the sudden, intrusive lump in my throat. "Maybe it's the opposite?" My voice sounds high to my own ears.

His eyebrows shoot up, but he doesn't respond immediately.

I rush to fill the empty space. "I'm scared I'll never pull the trigger. What if I keep holding back forever, and things get worse with the medical director and the pressure will keep on building and—won't that make it more awkward, and I don't—I don't want it to be this forced thing and—"

He stands and sets his coffee on the end table. In two strides, he's standing in front of me, and he cups my face in his hands. "Sadie, you are overthinking this, love." He kisses me lightly on the nose, and looks deep into my eyes. "I know it's hard, because of the circumstances that brought us together, but you have to put all of that aside when it's just us. There's no outside pressure, there's no genetic testing, there's no deadline, there's no population responsibility. There's you,"—he kisses my nose again—"there's me,"—his kiss lands on my cheek—"and that's it," he whispers and places his last kiss right on my barely parted lips.

My brain blanks out at his kiss, and the anxiety flows out of me in a rush. *Is it really that simple? Can I really let go of everything and be in the moment with him?*

He pulls back, and his thumb lazily strokes my cheek, lulling me into quiescence. I search his handsome face for any signs of discontent but find none.

"Now, my beautiful wife, would you like to go get some breakfast with me?" He holds out his hand in invitation.

I take his hand, and he leads me out of the cabin, and out of my uncertainties. In my heart, I know I'd follow this man anywhere.

Breakfast is uneventful, but tasty. Afterward, we are scheduled to go sailing in the harbor with Teddy and Faith, so we grab jackets from the cabin and head to meet them at the front of the guest house.

"I think we need to tell your brother and Faith who I am. I know we got interrupted last time on the hike, but, if the informant who leaked our marriage news is able to find my identity or location, we wouldn't be safe here. I would not be able to forgive myself if they were caught up in my own personal maelstrom." His hands are in his pockets, and his eyes are downcast to the small grassy path.

"I agree, we should tell them today if we can. But, Patrick, there's nothing you can do if someone finds out we're here. Frankly, there's nothing Teddy and Faith can do, either. They're stuck here for at least her first trimester." I can't help but shudder remembering the day we toured the medical facility, and the medical director said that going home wasn't guaranteed, even then. My knee still hasn't completely healed from the cuts I got from the beach stones in my hasty escape from that particular dose of reality.

"I've been thinking that over, ever since we saw the news report yesterday. One of your brothers is in the NAA Police force, right? Maybe Teddy could call him and have him pull some strings. Make up a family emergency? Anything to get them back in Georada, and out of the line of crossfire." He grows silent as we continue around the side of the building.

"Yeah, Peter is. But, I don't think he'd be able to do anything. I'm not even sure what he does other than travel around on official business and look intimidating in camo."

Patrick snorts at my description. "Really? Well, hopefully Teddy has some ideas. But as soon as we've got a moment alone, we need to tell them. Warn them."

I hate the sadness that's creeped into his tone, as if he's some kind of pariah. "It'll be fine, Patrick. You're not in charge of everyone else, even if you are some fancy politician's kid." I give him my best saucy wink, and he shakes his head at my shenanigans.

We round the corner, and Faith gives us an excited wave from the front walk. "There you two are! I've been dying to tell you all about the test results!"

"I'd ask what held you two up, but I really don't want the details," Teddy drawls as he arches an eyebrow suggestively.

"Get your mind out of the gutter, Teddy. We went back for our jackets. And you know I hate mornings, so hush." I give him my best scolding look in response. I've really perfected it over the years of dealing with six brothers.

"Poor Todd-from-Mairmont here has been waiting for ten minutes!" He waves his hands as if it's the end of the world. "He's probably out of coffee by now, and everything." Teddy gives me a wink.

"Don't you worry, Mrs. O'Roarke, I'm a-okay," Todd cuts in helpfully. "Are you all ready to head to the harbor? It's beautiful weather today for sailing."

Faith latches onto my arm and drags me towards the shuttle door. "Ignore your brother, he wants to get a rise out of you. Now, about my tests yesterday. It's too early to actually see anything going on in there, but they ran a whole blood panel, and they said everything is GREAT!" Her excitement really brings out her latent New Texas twang, and I can't help but smile.

"Also, the medical director said it's perfectly normal to not feel much of anything yet, and I was so relieved to hear that. Oh! And, she gave me an entire bundle of expectant mothers' ebooks to read on my mini-tablet!"

Teddy cuts in, an urgent tone in his voice, "For the love of mama's biscuits, DON'T let her show you the pictures!"

The face he pulls makes me bust out laughing. I don't even ask, just give Faith a fist bump. "Didn't know you were such a weenie, Teddy!"

He shakes his head and makes a disgusted face. "Fine, don't listen. But don't blame me when you can never eat spaghetti sauce again."

I look to Patrick in confusion, but he shrugs. Faith and I take the front loveseat, and Patrick and Teddy settle at opposite ends of the one behind us.

She squeezes my hand so hard in her enthusiasm that the little bones in my hand grind together. "It's so amazing, Sadie. After all this time, it's like my own invisible miracle." Her other hand flutters down to rest on her still-flat stomach.

"I'm so happy for you, Faith. You are going to be an amazing mother. *Are* an amazing mother, already." I amend my statement, because the change in her was instantaneous.

"Oh Sadie, you just wait. It's the best feeling, really. You'll see!" She throws her arms around me, and I hug her back carefully.

"Okay, time to get you folks sailing. We should be there in about fifteen minutes, but let me know if you need anything in the meantime!" Todd says, upbeat.

Faith continues excitedly telling me all about HCG and beta indicators the entire drive to the small harbor where a gorgeous white sailboat awaits us. It bobs in the gentle waves, and the wind makes snapping sounds against the tightly rolled fabric of the sails as we walk down the dock and over to the gangplank.

"Have you ever been sailing before?" I ask.

She shakes her head. "No, but it sounded fun in the brochure. Oh, and we asked and they'll cater lunch for us, too! This is definitely my favorite honeymoon location so far."

"Only your favorite location, huh? Not your favorite honeymoon?" Teddy waggles his eyebrows at her.

Faith's laugh is instantaneous and bright. "Hmm, I don't know . . ." she says, giving him a cheeky smile.

"Woman, you'd better think carefully about what you say next." His tone is mock serious as he snags her from me, and wraps his arms around her waist.

"It's no contest. You're definitely my best husband yet." She taps him on the nose, and he leans down and steals her next words in a kiss.

I look away, overwhelmed by their intensity. Patrick takes my hand, now that Faith is otherwise occupied, and we walk to the edge of the boat. *Why is everyone else so capable of jumping into this, but I'm holding myself back? Is there something wrong with me?*

The captain of the sailboat greets us at the railing. "Good morning! You've chosen a lovely day for a sail. Allow me to help you." He extends his arm to help me traverse the watery gap between dock and boat.

I take his hand and step over, the motion of the boat hitting me as soon as my feet are planted on the deck. Patrick steps on after me, and a moment later Teddy and Faith have caught up and stepped onto the boat with us.

The captain makes quick work of untying all the lines and heads up to the top deck where the captain's area is located. In a few short minutes we're pulling away from the dock, and towards the open water. The breeze is stiff, and I snuggle with appreciation into my coat. Patrick's hand is warm in mine, and for the first part of the ride, we all lean against the railing and enjoy watching the deck hands busy at their work as well as the scenery.

A crew member comes over, and offers us all fluted glasses.

"I'm sorry, no champagne for me, I'm expecting!" Faith glows as she shares her news for the first time.

The crew member gives her a polite smile. "We know, ma'am. We've got strict instructions for all honeymoon resort participants to only offer sparkling cider or grape juice."

She gives him a smile in return and takes one of the stemmed glasses.

I force myself to speak as soon as the crewman is out of sight. "I'm so glad all your tests went well yesterday, and you're both healthy so far. There's something we need to talk to you guys about, too, that relates to your pregnancy."

Faith's brow furrows and she looks back and forth between Patrick and me with worry. "What is it? Is everything okay?"

I set my hand on her arm. "Yes, everything is okay." I glance at Patrick, unsure how to actually break the news.

He clears his throat. "It's actually me that needs to share," he says, giving my shoulder a light squeeze. "I haven't been fully honest with you two, and I'd like to rectify that. My last name isn't actually O'Roarke, and neither is Sadie's. My name is Patrick Royce, and my father is the prime minister of the NAA."

It's out there, blunt and open. Like ripping off a bandage, the sting takes a minute to register.

Faith's jaw drops, and simultaneously Teddy's clenches. He locks eyes with me. "Did you know about this? Before you married him?"

I worry my bottom lip between my teeth, and shake my head.

His expression goes from surprise to fury in that split second, and he stalks forward towards Patrick. "You mean to tell me that you married my sister under false pretenses, let her send all those other men home, and now you're springing it on her that you're from the most prominent political family in the

.

entire country? And what, she's supposed to smile and pose for the cameras with you now, like nothing happened?" He hasn't touched Patrick yet, but his posture tells me he wants to punch him. I've seen enough brotherly tussles to know he is *not* playing around. *This could get ugly, fast.*

"Teddy—" I start, but Patrick squeezes my shoulder again.

"Sadie felt the same way, when I told her. It is inexcusable for me to have kept it from her, but I've apologized and done my best to make it right. I don't expect her to be some political trophy wife, if that's what you're thinking. The reason I live under a false name is to distance myself from my father's political career. I have no desire to be the next prime minister or hold a political office."

Teddy's eyes narrow with menace and his voice is low. "You and I both know that there's more at stake here than deciding to run for office. They're voting in the courts right now about making you the first ever *prince* of the NAA. Do you know what that would mean for Sadie, for our entire family?"

This time, I cut in. "Teddy, that's enough." His gaze snaps back to me. "I know you're angry. Heck, I was mad enough to spit. But this is not in Patrick's control. He doesn't want to be a prince, he certainly didn't call the media, and that's not why we're telling you this. There's something more important."

"What could possibly be more important? You got a nuke button in your closet, too?" he drawled, accent getting thicker in his anger.

"Your family's safety. The media shouldn't have gotten hold of the information about Sadie's and my marriage. I have no way to know what other information they might find, or how they're getting it. My parents haven't reached out, which means the leak hasn't been located yet. If they find out where we are, this place is going to get swarmed with media, and possibly more kidnapping attempts." He pauses, and takes in my somber expression.

"Sadie is now both the only known genetically normal woman alive, and married to the prime minister's son. We are telling you this so you can pull any strings possible, and get transferred back home to Georada. Do you think your brother Peter could pull some strings, and get you both sent home?"

Faith's face drains of all color as the discussion progresses, and she places a shaking hand on the railing. "I think I need to sit down."

Teddy quickly wraps an arm around her waist, and we all walk over to the seating area in the middle of the deck.

"Faith, I'm so sorry, what can I do?" I sink down next to her and hold her hand between both of mine.

She smiles, but it doesn't reach her eyes. "Do you really think we're in danger?" Her free hand presses protectively against her lower belly.

I press my lips into a tight line and look to Patrick for that answer.

"I hope not, but I wanted you to know and be informed of the potential risk. While I hope nothing comes of it, I can't guarantee that." He looks grim.

"I think they're right, Teddy, we need to try to go back to Georada." Faith is solemn, but less pale at least.

Teddy nods, a tight expression on his face. "What about you, Sadie? I'm supposed to leave you here with a man who lied to you, who put you into danger, and run off home with my tail between my legs?" His face shows his internal struggle, the torture plain as day.

"Teddy, you may have come here for me, but you have so much more than me to concern yourself with now. Patrick and I are okay. I want Faith and the baby to be safe more than I want to keep you here with me." I try to load my voice with reassurance, but he's far from convinced.

"I'll make a few calls as soon as we get back to the resort." He acquiesces, but I can read the indecision and fury in the stiffness of his shoulders, and the white-knuckled grip he has on the back of the seat Faith's sitting in.

The sailing trip now lacks the sparkling appeal it started with, and Patrick finds a staff member and asks that they take us back early. The shuttle ride home is equally somber, the only chipper one Todd. Although, if the rest of us were drinking sodas the size of a small bucket, we'd probably be a little more cheerful, too.

As soon as Todd lets us off and starts to pull away, Teddy is all business. "I'm going to make some calls and get us transferred home one way or another. But Patrick, if anything happens to my baby sister because of you, I don't care who you are, you will regret the day you lied to the Taylors and brought harm to this family. You understand?"

I have never seen my lighthearted, jovial brother so cold and threatening. The change in him is jarring, and tears start to gather along my bottom eyelid. *This is my fault; I should have told him the first day. Then at least he would have known before the stupid news got wind of it.*

Patrick's voice is deadly calm in return. "Teddy, I swear to you that I will do everything in my power to keep her safe, just like I have from the day I met her. My name may have changed, but I have not. I hope you'll see that in time."

They lock eyes, and the tension builds for a long moment as they stare each other down. Teddy gives a terse nod, before coming over to hug me tightly to his chest. I hug him back so hard it might bust a few ribs on a lesser man.

"I don't feel right leaving you here, Sadie. We're going to figure something out so you can come home, too." He tugs once on my ponytail, the same maneuver he's done since I was a little girl chasing after him through the pasture back home, and a single tear makes its escape and trails down my cheek.

I hastily swipe it away. "I'm so sorry, Teddy. I should have told you the first day, and I know it's no excuse, but I didn't want to ruin things for you and Faith. You seemed so happy, and I knew you'd go into overprotective brother mode. I needed time to process it for myself." I scuff the dirt with the toe of my boot, and can't bring myself to meet his eyes.

He puts a finger under my chin and pulls my chin up. "Sadie Alice Taylor, this is not on you, and I don't want to hear another word on it."

I nod, and he releases me. Without another word, he leads Faith by the hand towards their cottage. She tosses a small wave at me over her shoulder before they disappear past the guest house.

NINE

INTENSIVE

It takes five days, but Teddy somehow manages to get a transfer put in place for him and Faith back to Georada, to the local pregnancy center. They do extensive testing for most of that time before agreeing to release her, so we don't see much of them. Patrick and I mostly stay in our cottage, watching old movies on the built-in TV, and baking too much. I'm practically itching to get out and ride a horse, but there are no horses on the property, unfortunately.

This morning, we're supposed to meet them for early breakfast before Todd takes them back to the airport for their flight home. I've put it off as long as I can, but I finally shut the closet door and walk to the living room where Patrick is once again waiting with a cup of coffee. This morning, however, I'm too torn up for it to feel domestic.

Patrick assesses my mood and gives me my space as we walk to the guest house. We follow the stepping-stone path to the front of the guest house, and round the corner to see Faith and Teddy already there, bundled in coats and surrounded by their bags. My stomach clenches tight as a fist at the sight.

I feel wooden, the cold wind biting my cheeks forgotten as I walk over and hug them both tightly, one last time as the shuttle pulls in. Todd hops out of the shuttle, whistling a snappy tune that is at odds with our gloomy moods. Patrick and Teddy stiffly shake hands, and then it's time. My eyes water, tears pooling dangerously close to the edge. Faith steps back, giving me a moment with Teddy.

"I'm going to miss you, baby sister. I didn't plan for it to turn out like this." His voice is tight, and I realize that I'm not the only one fighting tears.

"I didn't either, big brother. But you've got two very important people to take care of now. And it's time I learned to stand on my own two feet. I'll be okay, promise." I force a smile, for his sake. He shouldn't be torn up about this, when I'm the one who chose Patrick. In that moment, it hits me like an express train that our lives have irrevocably changed. When I left the ranch, I thought I was going back home the same woman I was when I left. Now, such a short time later, both mine and Teddy's lives have been altered permanently—no matter when I make it home, things will be different.

"You're stronger than you think, Sadie. Keep your head down, and come home soon. We'll be waiting for you." He gives me a bear hug, lifting my feet off the ground for a second before setting me back down.

They board the bus, and the doors snap closed behind them. I watch, hands held tightly around my middle as the shuttle pulls out of sight, the separation leaving a hollow ache in my chest that feels far more permanent than the first time I was parted from my family.

We go in for breakfast and see two piles of luggage inside the front door. "Whose do you think those are?" I ask Patrick.

"Maybe some new couples arrived this morning?"

"That would be nice." *It's still going to feel empty around here, without Teddy and Faith.*

We walk through the French doors to the dining room, and I spot a long table with three couples seated. My eyes skip over the surprising presence of Odette and Dominic, past Emmett and Carolina, and land on none other than Nell and her personal mountain of tattooed muscle, Atlas. My jaw drops open.

"Nell!" I half shout in my excitement, and she looks up.

"Sadie! I'm so glad to see you!" She jumps up from her chair, and I run over and hug her before I think better of it. She doesn't flinch away from the contact like she used to.

When I first met Nell at the shuttle to the NLC, she was thin, wary, and running from her past. After a few months of good friends and good food, her inner light is shining through like the sun. Time with Atlas doesn't seem to have hurt, either—the two of them are cozied up at the breakfast table like they've been together ten years, not two months. The tall, thickly muscled man looks like he could be a direct descendent of a Norse legend. And he owns a private security firm. I'm not *entirely* sure what that entails, but it's a pretty safe bet that you want to stay on his good side.

"I'm so glad to see you, too! What are you two doing here? I didn't know you were planning to come to Mairmont!" The words tumble out in a rush.

She grins. "We weren't really planning anything, but, we decided we'd like to see some familiar faces on our honeymoon. Although, where are Teddy and Faith?" She looks around as if they're going to be right behind us, and my heart sinks.

"They actually just left," Patrick says.

"What? Where'd they go?"

"Home. But, Faith is pregnant!" I say, my happiness for her shining through my pity party for myself.

"Already? That's amazing! Is she thrilled, or nauseous?" she asks, sitting back down.

"Pretty thrilled. They both are."

"Well, hopefully the rest of us won't be far behind them, pregnant and headed home," she says, optimistically.

Odette snorts. "That's highly unlikely. The sooner you realize that, the better."

"Really, Odette? They've been here an hour and a half. Could you keep your bitterness to yourself for once?" Dominic snaps.

She glares at him icily, before standing and leaving the table.

"I shouldn't have said that," he mumbles and slaps his napkin to the table before following her.

"Uh, trouble in paradise?" I ask, looking to Carolina.

She grimaces. "Yes. Apparently, their number is up. They're being sent to the RID today, so things are . . . tense."

Patrick cuts in, "I thought they'd only been here a few months? Why the rush to the Reproductive Issues Department?"

Carolina exchanges a look with Emmett before leaning in. "Their relationship has been . . . let's call it troubled. They were sent on an intensive retreat their second month, and apparently things still haven't improved. They were given the choice between another intensive this week, or referral to the RID for IVF. Odette jumped at the chance for IVF, to avoid more time alone with Dominic." She shakes her head, clearly judging the decision.

Emmett puts his hand over hers. "They've had a hard time, Carolina. Let's not speak badly of people who aren't here to defend themselves."

She rolls her eyes. "I appreciate the sentiment, Emmett. But haven't we all had a hard road? You can't make it through this as brittle as glass. You've got to be willing to give a little, or you'll break into a million pieces. Not one of us here hasn't been through something. Not a one." Her tone is firm, brooking no argument.

"Well, it's added a lot of pressure that his ex, Carla, is already pregnant with her match. They found out this morning she's having a little girl," Emmett adds.

"Sounds like we've missed a lot," Nell says, thoughtful.

"We should get together and catch up," Patrick says, an undercurrent I can't quite pinpoint in his tone.

Atlas eyes him with speculation. "Agreed. I'm sure we have a lot to discuss. Dinner?"

Patrick nods tersely.

Later that evening, Atlas and Nell arrive on our doorstep at the agreed-upon time. When I open the door, they're holding hands and the sight warms my heart by a few degrees.

"Come in!" I say and step to the side.

"So, these little cottages are super fancy," Nell says, wasting no time. "They may be little, but they've got a lot of extras."

"Yeah, they're nice," I agree as we settle around the dining table. Patrick finishes setting up the plates and the food we'd ordered from the dining room for the occasion.

We all dish our plates, and before I can take my first bite of mac and cheese, Patrick shocks me to my toes.

"Atlas, we need your help with a few things."

Atlas sets his fork down, food untouched. "What do you need?"

Patrick glances at me once before dropping the bomb. "We need your help to find Josephine. I have a guard friend, Glitch, who's done some digging into her records since she was taken out of the announcement at the NLC. She is logged in the system as being here, and pregnant. There's no marriage record, and as far as we can tell she isn't actually here. We took a tour of the medical facility, but they said there are no pregnant women on site. The only other couples are the two you met this morning."

Nell frowns. "How would she already be pregnant? And what happened with that Elijah guy, anyway?"

"That's what we want to find out. Glitch is supposed to call back tomorrow with a report, and I was hoping you'd use your expertise to help us find out what's going on here."

Atlas looks contemplative. "How can you be sure it's not a mix-up? Glitch could be looking at old information, or another woman's record."

Patrick shakes his head. "No, Glitch doesn't make those mistakes. He's as close to a tech genius as they come, and he's hacked into the main databases and flagged her to find this information. It's not in the normal system, which makes us think something else is going on here."

His eyebrows shoot up at that information, but his otherwise stoic features don't change. "I see. I'd be happy to help you sort this out. But I have to ask, are you sure you want to kick over this rock for one girl? NLC guards are a dime a dozen, and if you get blacklisted, you'll never work in the system again."

"I'm sure you're right, but this is more important. Josephine may be one woman, but that doesn't mean we can let this go. And there's one more thing—I'm not just an NLC guard. I'm Patrick Royce, the prime minister's son."

Nell's jaw nearly touches the table. "Shut the front door. Haven't you been all over the news all week? And, oh, my word, that means you're the mystery wife!" She claps a hand over her mouth in shock and grabs Atlas's arm with the other, who is unmoved by the declaration.

"Patrick, are you sure about this?" I ask, shocked myself that he's revealed his identity to two relatively new acquaintances.

"I'm sure. It's time we take this search to the next level, and I won't put anyone else in danger to keep my own secret. The time for that has passed." His shoulders are straight, his voice firm, and in that moment I see it—I see the man who could lead an entire continent.

Atlas looks thoughtful, the only motion in his giant frame the slight ticking of his jaw muscle. "There could be major political consequences to this. I'm not going to sit back and ignore it if we find something illegal happening, and your father has endorsed this program. Are you prepared for that?"

"He may have endorsed this program, but there's no way he'd endorse this. I refuse to believe he knows what's going on. And it's become clear to me that *something* more is going on." Patrick says, and I get a chill down my spine.

"I'll call some of my contacts later this evening."

Nell has finally recovered from her shock, and focused in on the seriousness of the situation, "What is it exactly that you think is happening? Do you think they've locked her up somewhere, since she caused trouble? There's already a facility for troubled women. They very well could have sent her there. God love her, she refused to go with the flow. I doubt that changed once the sedatives wore off," she says with a frown.

"Glitch checked there first. There is one facility where they send troubled women, but there is actually a very low number of women there. Most get released based on health grounds and sent home. She was not checked in there. Her records vanished from the normal system. If Glitch wasn't as . . . *talented* as he is, we wouldn't have any idea that she was here."

And willing to break the rules, I add internally.

"I'd like to speak to Glitch when he calls you. I think if we can pin down more about where he's getting his information, we'd have a better starting point for our search. There's no good reason for a woman's records to disappear if she wasn't released from the program."

"You don't think she's in danger, do you?" I ask, both relieved he agrees with us and troubled that he thinks something is going on.

"It's impossible to say, but if she's on site, they wouldn't do anything to physically harm her. They need her healthy enough to carry the pregnancy."

There's a whole lot of harm possible that isn't only physical. My mouth presses into a grim line.

"We'll find her, Sadie." Patrick squeezes my hand.

Nell picks up a rib and takes a big bite. "Y'all sure know how to honeymoon," she says around a mouthful.

I snort. "You can say that again."

The next day passes in a pensive blur. We go to Nell and Atlas's cottage down the beach to await Glitch's call. Unfortunately, all he has to offer is another blood test record confirming Josephine's pregnancy is progressing, and it's still stamped at the Mairmont resort. Atlas and Glitch talk tech for a few minutes before they end the call, but we're no closer to a lead on Josephine than when we started.

"It doesn't make any sense," I say after a few minutes of the men discussing the issue.

"What doesn't?" Patrick asks.

"They have her records on some hidden database, right? So, in theory, nobody here knows anything about her. The other couples haven't seen her, and we wouldn't know she was supposed to be here if it weren't for Glitch's special access."

He nods.

"Well, the records are a secret, so they have no reason to hide the location. That means she is here, but they can't have her here in the main house, or else someone at some point would have seen her. She'd be out with everyone else, and there'd be no point to hide her records. Didn't one of the guides tell us this place has nearly five hundred acres? Why so much space, with no activities that use it?"

Atlas's eyebrows furrow. "There are no activities on the grounds? No trails, no livestock, nothing?"

I shake my head. "No, I asked the first week if they had a stable, and I was told no, something about the location was incompatible. There are a few hiking trails, but not five hundred acres' worth. Most of the activities take place right by the beach, or off site. They've left everything else forested."

"You think there's another medical facility here, somewhere else on the property? Like, secret agent style?" Nell asks, seeming enthused by the idea.

"Maybe her records aren't the only thing they're hiding. Maybe they're hiding *her*."

"The idea has merit. Do you two have a map of the hiking trails?"

Patrick goes to retrieve them from our cottage, and when he comes back he flattens the map out on the coffee table so we can all see. Atlas retrieves a permanent marker and starts putting Xes on the map along the edges of each defined hiking trail, activity location, and main drive in and out of the property.

When he's done, there are two huge swaths of untouched woods on either side of the main entrance. "That's plenty of space to hide a building or two. I'll have one of my guys come out with a drone and do some targeted fly-bys. In the meantime, I think the four of us need to do a little exploring."

Ten

THE HUNT

T he four of us spend the next few days hiking every single trail the eastern side of the property has to offer, keeping eyes out for any offshoots or side trails that might lead to another medical facility. Each night, Patrick and I collapse, exhausted, into our bed. Each morning, we wake up entwined together. In sleep when my defenses are down, the man draws me in like a magnet. The fourth day is no different, except for the first time since we've been here, I wake up before Patrick. The days of vigorous exercise must have finally worn him out. I prop myself on one elbow, and take him in.

The sun from our window is playing over his relaxed features, and I reach over absentmindedly and push a lock of dark hair back from his tanned forehead. He turns his head towards me but doesn't wake. As I drink in his quiet magnificence, I can't help but turn our relationship over in my mind. We've been here a month now, living together under the same roof, and I can honestly say he's the same man I thought he was, before he told me his secret. As much as I have held him at arm's length, he's won me back over, day by day, never pressuring me. He's made finding Josephine his top priority, stood up to the medical director, and been kind and considerate. He opens every door for me, and is always attentive.

So why am I holding back from him? Is it really him, or is it this situation? The thought strikes me, and I can't let it go. Am I still keeping us apart because of what he did, or because I don't like the fact that control over my own life, over my own body, is being taken from me by this program? Would it matter if it were any other man lying in the bed next to me? We only have about two weeks left until my next fertile week starts, and the deadline is looming in the back of my mind.

I shake my head because *I don't want anyone else lying next to me.* Then I freeze, as if he might be able to pluck the admission from my wayward thoughts. Oh, my. I don't want anyone else, only him. That's terrifying. *What if he lies again? What if he's acting so perfect now, but the instant we take things to the next step, or I get pregnant, he changes?* The thought is troubling, and I flop back against my pillow. I don't think that will happen, but I didn't see it coming the first time, either. Can I trust my own judgment where he's concerned?

I lay there, mulling over it all for a while longer before he rolls and captures me. His arm wraps around my rib cage, and his ear nestles against my chest, right above my pounding heart. Staying still so as not to wake him, his warmth sinks into me in sharp contrast to the chill of the fall air in our room. I carefully wrap my free arm around him and play with the collar of his shirt. He smells nice, too. Masculine and woodsy and warm.

He stirs again, and this time reaches up to rub his eye with the heel of his hand. It's his turn to freeze, and I barely contain my laugh when his cheek moves slightly, checking where he's landed. He ever so slowly pulls back as if he'll escape without waking me, and the laugh breaks free.

"I'm sorry, Sadie, I didn't mean to invade your personal space." He's bashful, and it's cute.

"It's all right, you were asleep." I give him a small smile, and to my everlasting wonder, a blush creeps up his cheeks.

"We'd better get going! Atlas and Nell are supposed to meet us at the trailhead, and we overslept. Well, I overslept," he amends, and quickly shuffles out of the bedroom to the hall bath. I hear the door click softly behind him and get up myself.

We arrive at the trailhead to find a grumpy Nell, and an amused Atlas. She's leaning into his tattooed bicep, nursing a travel cup of coffee.

"We have got to start these excursions a little later in the day from now on. I know it's important, but I need my beauty sleep, okay? I thought honeymoons were supposed to be all about lying on a beach and lazy afternoons in bed, not all this action and adventure crap." She blows on the coffee and takes a sip. "Bah! Still too hot." She grimaces.

Atlas just smirks at her complaints.

"Sorry, Nell, we can start later tomorrow." I pat her on the shoulder, and she waves me off.

"I have some news from my team. One of the guys brought a drone out, and canvassed the areas we outlined. He did not get a visual on any buildings."

"Well, shoot. So all this freaking hiking is for nothing? Can we go back to bed then?" Nell interrupts.

"Nope, sorry. He didn't get a visual on a building; however, we still have a lead."

"What did he find?" Patrick asks, eagerness coloring his tone.

"It's not what he found, it's what they didn't want him to find. He searched seventy-five percent of the area without issue, and then something shot the drone down. The last thing the camera caught before it was destroyed was a black combat boot."

The only sound is of our boots crunching up the dried fallen leaves in the path as we all take in this new turn of events.

Patrick is the first to speak. "Was the area near one of the main roads? Every honeymoon resort and NLC has guards. They may have assumed it was being used to plan another kidnapping attempt."

"That was my first instinct as well, but he sent over the coordinates this morning. It's nearly dead center to a patch of unmarked woods on your hiking map."

A shiver rolls down my spine. "What is a guard doing in the middle of empty woods?"

"That's the million-dollar question," Atlas responds.

We walk for another ten minutes before Atlas stops and pulls the map out of the small pack on his back. He's marked a red X on the spot where the drone went down.

"That's on the other side of the grounds. So, this hike is probably a bust today," I say with disappointment.

"Not entirely," Patrick says, "This is our last hike on this side of the grounds. If we finish them all, we'll have a good reason to go further afield without raising suspicion. We take this hike today, and next week we focus on hiking that side."

"None of the trails go anywhere close to that area," I point out, unclear how more hiking is going to help us.

"I guess it's time to tell the staff about our latent love of camping," Atlas says drily.

Nell's only response is a weary groan.

That night the four of us share dinner with Emmett and Carolina in the dining room. I make it a point to go on at length about the beauty of the hikes, and how much we're looking forward to next week's itinerary. The conversation flows easily, and dessert is served—a lovely cheesecake with strawberry topping. I'm stealing the last bite off Patrick's plate when a sudden buzzing overtakes the table, followed closely by Merengue music emanating from Atlas's general direction.

"What the heck? Is this thing broken?" Nell shakes her wrist.

"Oh, no honey. That's your fertility alarm. Looks like you'll have to postpone your hiking adventures until next week, I'm afraid," Carolina says kindly.

Atlas figures out how to stop his blaring alarm, and silence falls over the gathering.

"Well, we'll see you guys later. Have a good evening!" Emmett excuses the two of them from the table, and they make a hasty exit.

"Well that was awkward," Nell comments. "What an obnoxious way to announce to everyone that my eggs are droppin'." She looks at Atlas and shakes her head.

"It's horrifying, isn't it?" I agree.

"Well, you two can still take the planned hikes the next few days, and we'll join you as soon as we're able." Atlas is straight back to business.

"Agreed. Well, we'll let you guys get to it," Patrick says, and I smack him on the arm, boggle-eyed.

"Really, Patrick? Get to it?" We leave the table with a final wave to a laughing Nell and Atlas.

We decide to sleep in the next morning, since it's only the two of us hiking today and it's been a long week. Despite the fact that we tracked no activity during fertile week, they still dropped off a pack of urine sample cups, and I'm supposed to use them every day until my period arrives. Knowing it's pointless, I've been doing it anyways. *Better not to rock the boat over every single thing.* By the time we're ready to go it's lunch time, so we head over for a leisurely lunch in the guest house dining room and to drop off my pee cup.

We enjoy a lovely lunch of salads with grilled chicken, fresh croissants, and whipped carrot butter. Several of the staff are watching the daily news behind the counter, but at least today they've got the volume down so we don't have to listen to it. However, I notice Patrick glancing over to it several times as we eat.

"What's got you so distracted today?" I prod him, snapping his attention from the screen for the fourth time in ten minutes. My salad is nearly gone, and I've polished off two croissants while he's barely touched his chicken.

"I'm sorry, it looks like they've moved the monarchy bill up to a vote sooner than expected. I know there's nothing I can do, but I can't stop watching regardless. It could be any day that the vote will be over." The strain in his voice breaks my heart.

I reach over and grab his hand. "We just need to get your mind off of it. Do you still want to hike today, or do you want to go back to the cottage and take a day off? I can kick your butt at Scrabble again, if that would help," I say, giving him a cheeky grin.

"Okay, Mrs. Smarty Pants. You didn't kick my butt; you beat me by a few points. But no, we should hike still. We'll have a Scrabble rematch later." He smiles, and it's nice to see him distracted from the political storm that's brewing.

He finally eats, and we head out for the day. The nip in the air is more pronounced with each week that passes; before long these hikes won't be comfortable in a light jacket. *Hopefully we find Josephine before it snows.*

We've been walking for nearly an hour when something hits me. "Patrick, Atlas's drone was shot out of the air by a guard. What are we going to do when we run into those guards? Play dumb? There's no reason for us to be so far off the beaten path, and they'll be suspicious."

"Yeah, we need to *not* run into the guards if at all possible. That's also part of the reason we're hiking every trail. That way, if we are caught when we start to stray, we can say we were out looking for new areas to hike. I'm also hoping that there will be enough traffic near the area that we might be able to spot a small trail to follow. If there are guards, there is traffic in and out of the area daily."

He makes a good point. Those guards have to eat, and do shift changes, and go home like everyone else. Thinking of the logistics, the nagging worry of what will happen to the four of us if we're caught rears its ugly head, again. I force it down for the hundredth time. The urge to run away and find safety is strong, *but I won't give up on Josephine.*

"Don't worry, we're nowhere near the area today. We're saving the hikes closest to those coordinates for the end of the week when Atlas and Nell can join us again. So, these hikes are just for fun." He grins at me, and I appreciate his lightheartedness despite all that's going on. No matter what's been thrown at us, Patrick stays positive. And he supports me. *He really is a great guy.*

"Thank you for helping me look for Josephine. I know you didn't really know her, but I can't let it go. I need to know she's okay, one way or another."

He stops in the middle of the trail, and turns to face me. "Sadie, you don't have to thank me for doing the right thing. I agree with you, something weird is going on here. It would be irresponsible for us to not try to find out. I might have to lead this whole country one day, and how can I claim to have people's best interest at heart if I let women vanish out of a government-sponsored program?"

"There are tons of people in office right now who aren't here in the woods with us hunting down a single woman. You're going above and beyond, whether you think so or not." *Not to mention, someone higher up had to approve of whatever is going on here.*

He runs an agitated hand through his hair. It's gotten longer since we met, and he's starting to get a floppy, boyish look about him. "Haven't you figured it out yet? I'd do anything for you. Go anywhere, be anything you need. You've got my heart in your hands. I love you, Sadie. I know I haven't told you yet, but I'm trying to show you, one day at a time. I meant it when I said I would regain your trust. I will work until the day I die to be the best man I can for you." His gaze is piercing, and my breath catches in my throat.

He loves me? Warmth floods my heart at his admission. I stare back into his deep blue eyes, and in that instant something inside me clicks into place. "Can I ask you something?"

"Anything."

"You said—" I pause, suddenly nervous to ask the question that's eating at me.

"Please don't be afraid. You can ask me anything, tell me anything. I meant what I said. So, let it out, whatever it is." He takes my hands in his, and a crisp breeze plays with the ends of my braid.

"You said until the day you die. Did you mean that? You want this marriage to be long term, not just the three-year requirement? I'm not a political wife, Patrick. If you don't get made a prince this time, there's a good chance you will next time. I'm not cut out to be a queen. But, I'm having a hard time going all in if this is only going to be temporary. I need to know . . ." I swallow hard. "I need to know if I have to protect my heart, or if I can trust you. Forever." My voice is barely a whisper at the end, and I drop my eyes to his chest.

He's quiet for a moment, and my racing heart skips a beat when he drops my hand.

Oh, no, please don't tell me you want to divorce at the end—

His hand is gentle as it cups my cheek. "Sadie, please look at me."

I force my eyes up to his, and I'm sure he can read my fear and uncertainty plain as day.

"I am in this with you for the long haul. One hundred percent, every day, every hour, every minute of the time I have left—I want it to be with you. You have turned my whole world on its end, and I wouldn't have it any other way. When I wake up next to you in the morning, I feel like the luckiest man on this earth, and when I fall asleep next to you, it's with a smile on my face. I don't want to pull you into a political life you don't want. But I want you, and I'll do anything it takes to keep you by my side." His voice rings with sincerity.

Tears brim over, and I can't stop them. I suck in a gasping breath, so overwhelmed by his words that I don't even know how to respond.

"Hey, hey, please don't cry. I don't ever want to make you cry, my love." He swipes at the tears trailing down with his thumbs, and then plants a kiss on my cheekbone. "It's okay if you don't feel the same way, this is still new between us."

My heart wrenches at that, and I finally find my tongue. "That's not it. I—" The tears are coming faster now, but I fight through it to tell him what's in my heart. "I want to be all in, too. I want you, too. I—I love you, too."

The biggest smile I've ever seen crosses his face, and his joy shines so brightly that he eclipses the sunshine on this cloudless day.

"You love me, too?" He kisses my forehead and wraps both arms around me, pulling me against his chest so tightly I can barely breathe.

That gets a laugh out of me. "Patrick, I need some air, please."

He chuckles and loosens his grip but doesn't let me go. I go up on my tiptoes and press a kiss firmly to his lips. I can tell he's surprised, probably since I was crying. The tears have dried now, though, and I've got something else on my mind. I wrap my hands around his lower back, and pull him in tightly this time.

He kisses me back with matching fire, and I feel a rush of tingles from my head to my toes. One of his hands wanders up and threads into my hair, and I turn my head to deepen the kiss. We stay locked together like that for a long moment before he pulls back, a regretful look on his face.

My chest is heaving, heart pounding like a drum. "What's wrong?"

"I know we need to stop; I don't want to push you. I am so, so grateful you've given me a chance." He gives my arm a light squeeze.

I step forward again, invading his personal space, and put both hands on his warm chest. "I don't want to stop. I want you to kiss me again."

His eyebrows shoot up. "Are you sure? We're in the middle of nowhere, and we can take our time. There's no rush."

I pull his face down to mine, and kiss him again, letting my actions speak. He threads one hand back into my hair, and shrugs the pack off of his shoulder before gripping my waist tightly with his other hand. A few more heated moments pass in a blissful blur before he pulls away with a groan.

"Sadie, I need to stop. If we don't stop, I'm going to want to take things further—and our first time shouldn't be out here in the woods with nothing but a picnic blanket." He gestures to the beautifully colored trees lining the quiet path.

"You're wrong." My voice is quiet but firm. "This is better. It's just you and I; no politics, no pressure, no blinking resort lights or cha-cha alarms. You and me, as we are right now."

His eyes darken as I tell him what I'm thinking. He grips my hip again, and a thrill shoots through me at the possessive touch. "Are you one hundred percent sure? This is what you want, right here, right now?"

I step back into his chest, and slip my hands under the hem of his t-shirt. He sucks in a breath, but doesn't move. *He's going to make me say it.*

"I'm sure."

The fire in his eyes makes me forget the cold, forget everything but him in this all-consuming moment.

ELEVEN

FRIENDS IN LOW PLACES

T hree days later I'm settled in the chaise lounge in our room, a throw blanket in my lap and a cup of fresh cocoa from Patrick in my hands to ward off the chill as night falls. Life with Patrick is beyond anything I expected coming into this program. I was afraid I'd get matched with someone who was my opposite, who I clashed with, who I couldn't come to love and respect. Patrick is my opposite in many ways, sure. But, I have already developed so much appreciation for his kindness, determination, and the fact that he's down to earth. If I didn't know better, I would still believe he was Patrick the NLC guard, nice guy on an average path.

At first, I thought who his family is detracted from his ability to be a good fit for me as a husband; but as time goes on, I see how well we fit. It is even more amazing to me that he is so real, so *him*, despite the pressure and attention he's fought off for years with his father's job. *Hopefully Teddy will see it that way too. Eventually.*

A rock settles in my gut. The way things unfolded with Teddy is something I regret deeply. I've started and crumpled at least ten letters to him, since they left for home. *I am going to write it tonight. Whatever comes out, I'm sending it, no matter what. I* let my own embarrassment get in the way of honesty, and that's not something that's ever happened to me before.

I set the blue-patterned mug down, and pick up my pen again.

Teddy,

I am so sorry I didn't tell you sooner about Patrick. The truth is, I was ashamed. When I left home, everyone was so supportive and so sure I'd come home with the perfect husband to fit right back into life at home. And, I thought I did just that. But when he first told me, I felt foolish. A little girl playing at grown-up things. And I was too embarrassed to tell you.

I'm so sorry that I didn't give you the same time I took to get to know Patrick, and see that he is the same person I thought he was . . . more, actually. Because it's true, Teddy. He is so much more. I know that you're angry with both of us, but I hope that in time you will give him another chance. Because, the truth is, I love him. I've forgiven him, and I hope one day you will be able to forgive him, too. And me.

I hope you, Faith, and the baby are doing well—it's not the same here without you.

Miss you,

Sadie

It's not perfect, but it's sincere. I fold the letter and stuff it into a stationery envelope along with the one to Mom and Dad, and the other one for the rest of my brothers. I haven't gotten any return mail, but I'm not surprised given the seclusion they're so adamant about enforcing here.

Patrick walks in with a dish towel over one shoulder. "How's it going in here? Need a refill?" He points to my cup, which is still half full.

"No, thank you. It is delicious though. Are you ever going to tell me the secret ingredient?" I take a long sip, but the flavor eludes me.

He grins. "Sorry, I only have so many things I can make better than you; I have to keep that one to myself."

A fervent knock on the front door interrupts our domestic moment. A frown takes over my face. "Are we expecting Atlas and Nell tonight?"

Patrick shakes his head. "Stay here, I'll go see who it is." He reaches to the waistband of his pants, and I'm surprised to see he's got his pistol already tucked there.

He shuts the bedroom door, and I hear his footsteps down the hall, and the sliding of the lock on the front door. It's quiet for a beat.

"Sadie, come out! We've got a visitor." His voice is excited, so hopefully it's a good visitor. Not an angry-Melissa visitor.

I quickly drop the blanket and shuffle on my cold toes into the hallway, to see Glitch standing right inside the front door. "Glitch! What are you doing here?" I cross the distance between us and give him a brief hug.

He freezes, and then recovers and pats me on the back.

"Sadie, nice to see you again. You keeping this one in line?" He pokes his thumb at Patrick.

Chuckling, I say, "Yep, it's a hard job, but somebody has to do it."

"Ha-ha. I'm right here, and we're fine. But really curious what made you fly all the way up here from Georada. Is everything okay?" Patrick's tone drops as he gets straight to business.

Glitch's mouth pulls to one side in uncertainty. "I'm not sure. This whole situation has really been getting under my skin. I hate a mystery that I can't solve, you know? Oh! Hold on, before we chat." He fumbles in his pocket for a moment, and pulls out a round silver device no bigger than a coin with a single blue button on top. He presses the button, and continues, "Just a little signal jammer, in case there are any would-be eavesdroppers," he says, looking with a raised eyebrow at the ever-present band on my wrist. "But, anyways. I had a thought—Josephine is just one loud-mouthed woman."

I scowl at his classification of her, and he stammers.

"Sorry, Sadie, not in a bad way. Go with me for a minute?"

Patrick puts a comforting hand on my shoulder, and Glitch continues.

"Okay, so, Josephine is *one woman*, right? She can't be the only one who's been upset enough about a match—or about the rules of the program—to speak up, right?"

We both nod, unsure where he's going with this line of thought.

"Well, that made me think, maybe she's not the only woman who's disappeared, either. Most NLC groups each quarter are small, one or two women at a time. Occasionally three. So, there are way less witnesses to the kind of thing that happened to Josephine, usually, and no one to follow up. So, I started digging around looking for other pregnancy records *not* in the main system. It was a dead end at first, because there are still women who, until the latest emergency mandate, were out there, you know, living lives with their hubsters and having the occasional baby in the wild, so to speak. Did you know that the NLC still tracks all of those? I don't think they're supposed to have that data."

"Glitch, my man, get to the point, please," Patrick interjects.

"Sorry! Right! Anyways, that was a dead end, because those women are living their normal lives. Then I narrowed it down to pregnancies in the right age range to be in the Compulsory Marriage Program, but NOT associated with a marriage record. And I hit paydirt." He starts digging in his backpack, and pulls out a thin tablet. He taps a few times, and then flips it around so we can see a spreadsheet, full of names.

"What is this list?" I ask, dreading what he's about to say.

"This list is eleven more women, all with pregnancy records, all listed in Mairmont, with no associated marriage record. That's just the beginning," he says, as my stomach drops to my feet. "Once I figured out what search criteria to run the queries on, I found women listed all over the NAA that match it. There is a group of women in almost every single tri-state. And because I'm sure you'll ask, I checked, and these are not registered detention facilities. There's only one of those, over in Colkanska. And most of those women get discharged without getting married or pregnant."

"That's . . . That's a *lot* of women. How are all these women pregnant but not married?" I ask the first thing that jumps out at me. "Wait, and you said there are eleven more here, in Mairmont?"

He nods. "Yep, there are. The groups vary in size from tri-state to tri-state, but the one in York has over twenty. The smallest one I found is only three, up in Saskerta. Their population is struggling more than most, though, so it's not surprising."

Patrick's face is angry when he finally speaks. "What in the devil is going on, Glitch? We're both pretty familiar with the NLC guidelines, and I can't think of a single law that would allow all these women to be pregnant outside of marriage. And why have them all at secondary locations? There definitely aren't twelve rooms full of pregnant women in the main guest house, and on my morning runs I've only seen six couples' cabins total."

"I don't know, Rick-Raff. I think we've stumbled onto something here, and I don't think it's good. That's why I came in person; I think this goes beyond Josephine getting into hot water, and I didn't think it would be wise to discuss it over the phone." His voice grows serious, for the first time since I've known him.

"Glitch, if all these women aren't married, is there any record of who the babies' fathers are, or how long they've been where they are?" I ask.

"I haven't found that information yet because it's probably stored in a separate database. You know, they rarely store top-secret stuff all together like it's wrapped in a bow. But I can do some more digging." He takes the tablet back out of my cold fingers, and immediately starts tapping out notes, like we aren't even there.

"Take a load off, man. Want some coffee?" Patrick points him towards the couch.

"Yeah, coffee's great," he mumbles, already lost in his hacking efforts.

I frown and follow Patrick into the kitchen, where he's already starting a fresh pot of coffee. "Patrick, I have a really bad feeling about this. There's no good reason to have all these women hidden away."

He presses *brew* on the pot and turns to face me. "I agree, Sadie, but we're getting closer to figuring this out. All we can do is keep searching and try to figure out where they are."

"Patrick, there are over twenty-five tri-states. Even if most groups are on the smaller side, that's a *lot* of women. Who's hiding them? Are they being treated well? Are they going to get to go home once their pregnancies progress past the first trimester, like a normal pregnancy in the marriage program?" My mind is running a thousand miles a minute.

"I wish I knew," he says and pulls me against his chest. I breathe in his comforting scent, and send up a silent prayer for answers, soon. This is all turning out to be much more than picking the right honeymoon destination.

The next day, after Glitch snuck back out of the resort grounds to do more research in the closest town, we meet Nell and Atlas by the final trail head for the marked hiking trails at our resort. After this, we're going to start branching out further into the woods towards the coordinate given to us by Atlas's employee with the drone. So far, no trail has had any unmarked side paths, or anything indicating there's traffic towards that portion of the woods.

Once we're far enough into the trail that no one could overhear, we catch them up on what Glitch shared last night, before he spent three hours working on our couch and passed out, still clutching his tablet.

"I'm sorry, but if there's another branch of the program that is this big, how has word not gotten out? Wouldn't their families tell, or wouldn't it be obvious when they go home with a couple of kids but without a husband? Although, I guess they could set them up as divorcées," Nell muses.

Atlas is quiet, the only sign he's unhappy with this information is the ticking muscle in his jaw, visible even under his five o'clock shadow.

We all walk in silence for a while, pondering the potential ramifications of this information. Eventually, Atlas stops walking.

"Right there." He points, but all I see is more trees and underbrush.

"What is it?" Nell asks, wrapping her hands around his bicep and trying to get even with where he's pointing.

"It's another trail. It doesn't connect to this one, but there's a definite break in the underbrush."

"That's not a game path, either," Patrick agrees. "It looks like it's a gap barely wide enough for an ATV. Maybe for guard shifts?"

"Let's go check it out." Atlas shrugs off his pack and hands it to Nell, and Patrick hands his to me. They wade into the scrub, and I don't envy them the scratched-up shins they're going to have after this. Nell and I look at each other nervously, despite the fact that the area is deserted apart from the four of us.

After they make it through the scrub, they find what must be the break in the woods. It doesn't look too different to me, but I'm no expert. They continue walking out of sight, and we can no longer hear the sounds of their footfalls.

"We should set up our lunch, so at least we're doing something other than just standing here," Nell suggests.

"We should have gone with them," I mutter, but open the pack in my hands and pull out the picnic blanket. I blush at the sight of it, but quickly shake it off.

"So, did you two have fun hiking by yourselves last week?" she asks in a bland tone, and I try not to choke on air. Thankfully she doesn't notice. "Because frankly, I enjoyed a few days of hanging out at the cabin and doing nothing. Well, mostly nothing," she amends and gives me a wink.

"I don't want the details!" I rush to interrupt, which makes her laugh.

"You are such a prude. But don't worry, I wasn't going to give you the nitty gritty." She waggles her eyebrows at me, and hands me a bottle of water before sitting cross-legged on the blanket.

"Thanks." I hand her a sandwich and a fruit cup.

We sit and munch, scanning the woods for our men. As the time goes on, my unease grows at the separation. What if something happens to them, or they get caught? We'd be stuck sitting here biding our time all afternoon, no idea when to expect them back. *Next time, we're all going. Waiting around like this is for the birds.*

Finally, when the sun is directly overhead, we hear the sound of footsteps approaching from the direction they'd gone. Nell and I stay seated, but keep our eyes trained on that spot in the woods where they'd vanished. I let out a huge sigh when I see Patrick round a corner in the path, and a moment later Atlas appears behind him. Nell and I exchange relieved glances.

"Well, neither of them look like they got shot, so that's a good sign," Nell says, her light tone not in line with the seriousness of our worries.

It takes a few minutes, but the men tromp back through the thick brush and flop down on the picnic blanket with us.

"Well, what did you find?" I ask, unable to wait a second longer.

Patrick shakes his head. "Just a guard shack, I'm afraid."

"Ugh, you guys were gone for at least two hours, and the only thing over there is a guard shack?" Nell complains, and my disappointment echoes hers.

"So it's another dead end?" I ask. *Where the heck are these women?*

"I wouldn't call it a dead end. We were able to observe some of the guard patterns for a short span, and there is definitely activity on the other side of the guard shack," Atlas says.

"Yeah, we saw them taking a trail on the other side, which doesn't lead to anything on the map. We're getting close, I can feel it. They have to be over there." Patrick adds as he takes the sandwich I offer him.

"So, what now? Do we hike past the guard area and try to find the trail?" The idea is daunting, but I don't see what other option we have.

"Can I request an option where we don't spend all day freezing our butts off in the woods? It's getting a lot colder, and I'm sick of all this hiking. Blah blah, nature—it all looks the same at this point," Nell cuts in.

"Actually, I had an idea," Patrick says with a smile. "We're going to ask for some ATVs. The guards had a few, and we think we could make it through the brush with one. It's going to be a lot faster and we'll cover more ground."

"I'm not complaining, because my blisters have blisters at this point. But how exactly does the guards having ATVs help *us* get them?" Nell points at the four of us.

"We're just going to *suggest* a new activity to the program director," Atlas says nonchalantly and takes a huge bite of his sandwich.

TWELVE

MONARCH

Atlas and Patrick pulled some strings with the program director, which I suspect might have involved Atlas volunteering to donate the ATVs for the new activity. He approved it, no questions asked, but the ATVs are taking a few days to get shipped here. In the meantime, we're trying to recoup from our nearly two solid weeks of hiking. The rest is nice, but worry for Josephine and all the other women on that list keeps niggling at the back of my mind, and I find myself more and more restless as the days pass.

The increasing cold combined with that restlessness is what's driving us to loiter in the guest house today, waiting for Nell, Atlas, Emmett, and Carolina to play a card tournament with us. The staff have put out a nice spread of finger foods, which I'm enjoying heartily, much to Patrick's amusement.

"I don't know how you eat that stuff. It doesn't have any resemblance to real meat," he says, and wrinkles his nose at my selection of sausages stuffed into bacon, bread, and shaped into balls.

"You don't have to understand it. You clearly have no appreciation for life's delicacies," I say with a smug smirk.

He chuckles and gives me a kiss on the head, and slides his hand into the back of my jeans pocket. "You're kind of weird, but you're *my* kind of weird," he says.

Now it's my turn to scrunch up my nose at him. "I'm not sure if I should be offended or happy about that," I say before popping another sausage-wrapped-in-bacon into my mouth happily.

"What's up, newlyweds!" Emmett sounds jazzed as he and Carolina make their way in. High fives are exchanged all around before they grab some snacks of their own.

Atlas and Nell arrive a moment later, and we all settle down to play some cards. Emmett is the most serious I've seen him, as he explains the rules to us. Most of it goes over my head, having never been much of a card player. But I've got snacks and friends, so I don't mind losing for the cause.

After three rounds of being the first to lose, I make my way back to the buffet for seconds. Seeing that everyone else has started a fourth round, I ask one of the ever-present staff, Jerome, if he would set up a movie for us in the conference room. I give Patrick a quick wave, which he sort of acknowledges through his intense focus on his hand, and follow Jerome across the hall to see what our options are. I choose an action and adventure flick, and Jerome shows me how to turn on the movie with a built-in panel in the wall—when everyone is tired of their cards. While I'm waiting, I switch on a Christmas movie. I know it's early, but who's going to stop me?

I'm really invested in the plucky heroine's quest for Christmas love ten minutes later when the screen cuts out.

"Shoot, what happened to my movie?" I ask no one in particular, right as Candy Thomas from NAA One takes over the screen. "Aw, come on! I need to know what happens to Raquel!" I grouch, but quickly fall silent at the familiar blonde anchor's announcement.

"We're coming to you live this evening, pausing your regularly scheduled programming with breaking news across the entire North American Alliance." Candy pauses for effect and looks gravely at the camera before speaking again. I cross the room to turn up the volume on the wall panel.

"Today, at 8:40 p.m., the justices across the North American Alliance have voted to uphold the bill enacting a monarchy. Prime Minister Royce has simultaneously accepted the nomination to become the first ever king in the history of the NAA. We're expecting a live update from newly appointed King Royce any minute now."

My jaw drops, and my head spins with this news. *I have to go get Patrick.* I race across the hall, back to where the others are still engrossed in their cards, blissfully unaware of what's unfolding outside these cloistered walls.

"Patrick, can you come here, please? It's urgent." Something in my tone must convey my inner turmoil, because he pushes back his chair in a heartbeat.

"What's wrong, are you okay? Are you sick?" He puts his hands on my shoulders.

"No, I'm fine. Come with me." I grab his hand and haul him to the conference room, where the news anchor has disappeared, and a press conference is starting. The podium is empty, but people are filling up the stage in anticipation of the speech that's about to begin.

"Oh, God. Is it the vote? Do they have the results already?" He grips the back of one of the chairs, knuckles white.

"Yes, they did," I say softly. I know I need to tell him, but how do you break that kind of life-altering news? I hadn't thought that far ahead when I ran to get him. "Patrick, the vote. They—"

He tears his gaze away from the screen, and as soon as he takes in my expression, he knows. The color drains from his face. "It's done. They passed it." His voice drops low, anguished.

Nell's head pops around the door frame. "I don't want to intrude; just wanted to make sure everything is okay? We're all worried."

"We're fine, thanks for checking on us, Nell." I give her my most reassuring smile.

"Uh-huh. Are you pregnant? Puking? Lose a limb?" she rattles off.

"No to all. Can you give us a few minutes, please? We're fine." I make a shooing gesture.

She shakes her head but backs out of the door and shuts it behind her.

"I'm sorry, Patrick. I know this is not how you wanted things to go." I scoot myself under his arm, and wrap him up in a hug. We stay like that, him hugging me back tightly, until a stately woman with cinnamon hair streaked with silver walks out, her smile beaming warmly from ear to ear, followed closely by the prime minister, his father.

"That's my mom," he says, voice hardly above a whisper as his father takes the podium.

"Good evening, citizens of the NAA. I stand before you this evening both humbled and honored, as your representatives, as a nation, have once again put such faith in my capabilities as a leader, and my family's commitment to keeping this country strong, and growing—now and for future generations." He pauses, and looks into the camera as if he's looking directly into my eyes. He portrays sincerity and humility in equal measure, and it's no surprise to anyone why he was chosen. "I know this will be a time of great transition, but I urge you all to continue in hope for what's to come. We will come together as a nation, as a people, and continue to fight the detrimental effects of the Sterilization Vector on our great lands. Together, we will continue to rebuild, and our children's children will inherit our vision. Thank you all. Good night." He raises a hand in a gesture, and the press begins to vie for his attention, but he merely waves, and my prim, suited mother-in-law gives a soft wave to the crowd before taking his arm and together they exit the stage.

The news anchor pops back into the frame, but I go and turn the panel off. We've seen enough.

Returning to Patrick, I take in his stiff posture. He doesn't say anything, doesn't move, and keeps staring with a blank expression at the darkened screen. I can tell this is going to take a while to sink in, so I hug him again and settle in to wait.

The next morning, we're startled awake by another unexpected knock at our cottage door. I rub my bleary eyes, and see that it's only seven a.m. "Who in the world is knocking at this hour? Don't they know people need sleep?" I say, and pull my pillow over my head to block out the intrusion.

Patrick chuckles, and tickles my knee before he goes to answer the door. *Morning people, ugh.*

I hear voices muffled by my pillow, before the bed dips and Patrick climbs back in and pulls me into his side. Grudgingly, I lower my pillow, and see that he's holding an envelope.

"Who's it from?"

He slides out a letter and quickly scans it. His hand lowers, and a neutral expression crosses his face. "It's from my mom." He slips it into my hand.

Patrick,

I trust you've heard the news regarding the recent change to our family's status. As such, we ask that you please keep a low profile until an appropriate security detail can be put in place for you. We will have it arranged as promptly as possible.

Yours,

Deb

"Is this the first time you've heard from her since we got matched?" I ask, stunned by the lack of affection in the missive.

He nods.

"That's it? It's so cold. She doesn't even sign it Mom, just Deb?" I scan the letter again, searching for any sign of warmth. Heck, not even a congrats on the marriage? "She didn't say congratulations, or ask how you were." My annoyance at my new mother-in-law builds. She has to know Patrick is unhappy about the news, and yet there's nothing in there to try to comfort him, or even acknowledge his feelings. *Rude.*

"That's her. Brisk and to the point." He takes the letter back and tosses it onto his bedside table. "I think I need a run this morning. Will you be okay here on your own if I go out and clear my head?" He gives me a lackluster smile, nothing like his usual boundless cheer, and I hate to see how hard he's hit by this whole situation.

"Of course. I'll have breakfast ready when you get back." I pucker my lips, and he leans over and kisses me, but it's brief, with none of the usual heat I've come to expect between us these days.

Patrick's only been gone on his run five minutes when an excited pounding comes at the door. Assuming it's Glitch with some update for us, I hurry over only to find a windswept Nell.

"Sadie! We heard the news. So, you and Patrick are officially *royal* now. How does it feel? Do you get a tiara? Are you carrying a royal heir yet?" She gestures with wild enthusiasm at my unchanged midsection.

"Would you hush and get in here?" I grab her by the arm and haul her into the house. She doesn't protest, just walks right in, and sits on a bar stool. I look around, but thankfully our cottages are all well-spaced, and there's no one in sight to have overheard her.

"Have you got any cookies? Yours are way better than the ones in the guest house."

I shake my head at her presumption but pull a few cookies I'd baked yesterday out and put them on a plate for her.

She takes a huge bite before continuing. "So, I take it that you two weren't happy about the royal news last night?" A crumb falls out of her mouth and lands on the counter.

"No, not so much. Neither of us wants to be royal, or political. We just want . . . normalcy." I sigh. "But, I think that ship has sailed." I watch in morbid fascination as she grabs the errant piece of cookie with her thumb and pops it back into her mouth.

"Yeah, that's not really an option anymore. But, hey, why be normal when you can be a princess? You are a princess now, right?"

I don't answer, instead I cross to the fridge and pull out a bottle of milk and pour it into a short glass for her. Handing her the glass, I drum my fingers on the countertop restlessly. "It's all too fresh, Nell. I don't know anything yet, and I am worried about Patrick. He didn't take the news well at all—you should have seen him last night. It was the first time I've ever seen him look rattled."

"He is a pretty easy-going guy most of the time," she agrees while dipping her second cookie into the glass of milk.

"Yes, he is. When those kidnappers came to the NLC, he was cool as a cucumber. I don't know how to handle this side of Patrick."

"Well, to be fair, it's the first time you've seen it. We're all newlyweds, after all." She says it so matter-of-factly, it helps ease the tension in my shoulders.

I turn and grab a cookie for myself before answering, "You're right, this is all so new. I wish I knew how to help him. What to do, you know? So far, all I've done is bake everything in sight."

"It's okay, he's a runner. He won't lose his hot bod before the honeymoon's over."

"Who's got a hot bod?" Atlas's voice rumbles from the entryway, and I jump a mile high.

Nell spins on her barstool towards the sound of his voice, and gives him a salacious grin. "I'll never tell."

He smirks, clearly not concerned with her inspecting someone else's physique. "Oh, you'll tell. Or I won't let you drive," he says, waving a short key with a black rubber grip in front of her face.

"Ooh, does that mean they're here?" Nell claps her hands like a little kid on Christmas morning. In that moment, I'm reminded exactly how young she is.

Atlas nods. "When Patrick's back, we can take them for a spin. If you're done with your cookies, that is."

"I think I'm good; I had two. Although, one for the road wouldn't hurt." She turns back to me, and I hand her and Atlas each a cookie in a napkin.

"Those are the last two, so don't rush it. I'll make more later."

"Yes, *Mom*," she sing-songs back at me.

I'm shaking my head at her antics when I hear an ear-splitting boom break through the peaceful morning.

"What was that?" I ask, but Atlas is already in motion.

"Get in the bathroom, and lock the door. Don't open it unless Patrick or I tell you to!" By the time the front door slams behind him, Nell is already on her feet and around the counter. She grabs me by the wrist, and we race down the hall to the bathroom.

My hands shake as I lock the door, and another boom sounds close enough to shake the cottage.

"Get in the tub!" Nell urges, and we both clamber in.

"Why are we in the tub?" I ask, after we're in it. Thankfully it's a large soaker tub, so we both fit with our knees up.

"Extra protection from stray gunshots," she tells me, voice tight.

I reach out and grip one of her hands, and she squeezes mine back tightly. "I don't think those are gunshots, way too massive —the whole cottage is shaking. Did Atlas teach you that?"

"Yes, after the first kidnapping attempt. He was barking orders left and right and took me straight to my room and shoved me into the bathroom and told me to lay down in the tub until he came back. Good gracious, why do people keep trying to kidnap us?" She lays her head on her knees, and I'm not sure whose hand is shaking harder, hers or mine.

A third boom sounds, even closer this time. The tub rattles underneath us, and in the cacophony I almost miss the sound of the front door bursting open.

"Was that the door?" Nell's voice is a whisper now.

"I think so," I answer in a barely audible voice.

Heavy footsteps thud down the hall, and I hear the bedroom door open. The footsteps fade as the person goes deeper into the room.

That's not Atlas. There is a kidnapper in my house right now. My heart pounds against my ribs, and I can feel my breaths coming in shorter and shorter gasps. I try to stay silent, despite my imminent hyperventilation.

The footsteps return to the hall, and I hear the bathroom door knob turn once, twice. A muffled curse comes from the other side of the door, and I hear the crackle of the man's communication wristband. "Possible target in cottage three."

Nell's grip on my hand turns vice-like, and we both sink as far down into the tub as we can. Silent prayers pound in my ears with my pulse.

"Affirmative, pickup on standby," a different voice responds on the device.

Where the heck are Patrick and Atlas? Oh, God, I hope they haven't been shot. Or captured.

"Making entry," the muffled voice says, and then he backs up a few steps.

"Oh, Jesus," Nell breathes, and we make desperate, terrified eye contact.

The next instant the bathroom door crashes inward, and splintered debris comes flying into the tub onto our backs. I squeeze my eyes tightly shut on instinct, and hear the ear-splitting crack of a gunshot, followed closely by a loud thud.

All is silent for a heartbeat, then another. I open my eyes and force myself to look over the lip of the bathtub, and see our would-be kidnapper lying in a black-clad heap outside the bathroom door. I squeeze Nell's hand, and she takes in the scene with me.

The sound of running feet barely makes it to my still-ringing ears, and then Patrick appears in the doorway, as if by magic.

A grateful sob tears itself from my throat, and I take in his sweat-drenched running clothes, sharply contrasted against the sleek black rifle in his hand.

"Sadie! Thank God! Are you all right?" He steps over the prone form and reaches in to help Nell and me from the tub.

"I was so scared. I was so scared, Patrick!" I'm clutching his shirt, sweat forgotten, and see that Atlas has appeared and taken Nell into his arms as well.

"I know, sweetheart. I was scared too. But you're okay now, I've got you." His hand cradles the back of my head, and he sweeps his gaze along my form, as if checking for injuries.

"We have to move, it's not safe here." Atlas's brusque tone brooks no argument, and he heads straight out of the bathroom.

"There's no exterior door in there, Atlas," I point out, as he strides into our bedroom. One by one, we step over the black-clad man in the doorway, and I try not to notice the pool of blood spreading across the gorgeous wood floors.

"Don't need one." He throws open the window, and in one fluid motion steps onto the sill and leaps out. Nell is right behind him and scrambles out a moment later.

Patrick and I reach the window and see two shiny black ATVs parked right under the window. Atlas has caught Nell, and scooted her to the one furthest from the window.

"Go ahead, I'll be right behind you," Patrick says before crossing to his night stand, pulling something flat out of the drawer and slipping it into his pocket.

"Come on, I'll catch you." Atlas makes an impatient gesture, as I step up onto the sill. My foot slips, and I tumble out in a graceless heap. He catches me with a grunt, sits me on the second ATV, and then slides over in front of Nell and cranks their ATV. Patrick is beside me in an instant, silent as a cat. He slides in front of me, and with a kick, the ATV beneath us rumbles to life.

Atlas spins the tires as he steers the roaring ATV into the dunes behind our cottage.

THIRTEEN
BUTTERFLIES

I cling to Patrick's waist, and bury my face into his back as the wind rushes by, whipping my hair wildly around my face and ears. The cold metal of the rifle slung across his lap bounces against my knuckles whenever we hit a bump. I clutch him tightly, and pray as hard as I can for the kidnapping attempt to be over. *Where did he even get a rifle?*

Soon, the landscape around us changes, and the ground smooths out. After about 15 minutes, Patrick slows the ATV, and I finally lift my head to look around. The familiar autumnal foliage of a hiking trail surrounds us. Atlas and Nell are rolling slowly right next to us.

"This is the best chance we'll have to slip past the guard shack," Atlas says, voice raised over the sounds of growling engines.

"I agree," Patrick says with grim determination. "It's going to be much harder to investigate once my guard detail arrives."

Atlas gives a sharp nod, and then speeds off in front of us. Patrick follows hot on his heels, and I bury my face back into his shirt.

Time passes strangely as we ride down the cold trail. Every time my heart starts to slow to a normal pace, another loud explosion rocks the earth behind us, in the direction of the guest house. I watch the trees whip by in a blur, and my eyes water from the stinging wind. Eventually we slow again, and Patrick turns our ATV off the wide hiking trail and into the scrubby brush between the towering trees.

The ATV engines quiet to a purr as we slowly crawl through the underbrush. Thankfully most of the scrub bends beneath the tires, but I still get a few scratches along my chilled arms when things spring back up. We ride one behind the other until we reach the ATV trail to the guard shack. Atlas waits for Patrick to pull us up to his right.

"Stay low and be ready to cut the engine on my signal." His tone is sharp and to the point. With that, he pulls back in front of us, and we continue down the ATV trail at a moderate clip. After another five minutes or so, Atlas veers off the path and into the scrubby underbrush.

We continue on this circuitous route at a slower pace, and I think that I can just see a clearing in the distance that we seem to be skirting around. *That must be the guard shack.* Eventually we make it through the forest and see another trail, this one too narrow for us to ride side by side. Atlas stops and signals for Patrick to kill the engine, and they both climb off.

"Stay here, and stay low. If we tell you to take off, you take off. Don't look back, don't ask questions. Clear?" Atlas orders, and Nell and I both nod. Patrick shoulders his rifle before he and Atlas cross to the trail ahead. They disappear from sight, and the sounds of the forest envelop us. Nell and I exchange nervous glances, but we don't dare speak.

What feels like an eternity later, the soft snap of twigs alerts us to the men's return. A sigh of relief escapes me as I see Patrick's dark wavy hair appear, followed closely by Atlas's blond buzz cut.

They quickly climb back on in front of us. "We're clear. The guard shack looks deserted; this is our chance," Patrick says quietly before kicking the ATV back to life. This time, Atlas surges forward and the roar of the engine cuts through the forest like a knife.

We make a hard left onto the narrow trail, and within a few minutes we enter another clearing. There is some kind of screen across the entire top of the clearing, which makes it unnaturally darker than it should be without any tree cover. In the middle of the open ground sits a good-sized windowless white building. There are no signs or other markers to indicate its purpose, just a door with a square pad above the handle.

We all hurriedly dismount, and head straight to the door.

"It looks like it requires a keycard." Nell points to the pad above the knob.

"I should be able to get us in." Patrick slides in close to the door, and whips a nondescript white card from his pocket. "Glitch took my old guard card and wiped it and loaded it with every access code he could find. If this doesn't work, we'll have to try to break it down."

"What if this isn't the right place?" I ask, worried.

"It would be just perfect if we break down the door to a glorified broom closet." Nell's voice drips with sarcasm.

The pad lights up with a green outline and an innocuous chirp, followed by the click of the lock releasing.

"Glitch, my man!" Patrick quietly exalts.

Atlas steps back to the front, and pushes the door open. He peers around the door in silence, but pushes it open onto a bare, sterile white hallway. The overhead lights are harsh to my eyes compared to the dim screened exterior, and the sharp tang of disinfectant bites my nose.

We all pile into the hallway, and make our way down. I'm not sure what I expected, but this wasn't it. It's silent here, and appears empty. Halfway down, another hall splits off. Atlas stops, and gestures with two fingers down the side hall, and then the main hall. Patrick nods, and takes my hand. We split off down the side hall, while Atlas and Nell continue forward on silent feet.

A doorway is on the right. Patrick waves me past it, and gestures for me to wait. Rifle at the ready, he slips the doorway open and spins inside without making a sound. From my angle, it appears to be an office. I turn back to the hallway, keeping an eye out for anyone else that may be in here. Halfway down, I see what looks to be a large glass window set into the wall. Glancing over my shoulder to see Patrick rifling through papers on a desk in the empty office, I continue down the hall to check out the window.

I peer carefully around the edge, scared that there will be someone on the other side to spot our intrusion. What I see instead stops me in my tracks.

There are people in the room, but none that can sound an alarm. Instead it's two rows of hospital beds, each with a woman strapped into it. They lie there so lifelessly, in white hospital gowns that at first, I think they're dead. After a moment, the collective rise and fall of their chests registers and I suck in a relieved breath. I look past the window and see a door into the room. Crossing over to it, I shove my way in.

Thoughts of being spotted have left me, and all I can think about is finding out what is going on with these women. I cross to the first bed, and the pale woman in it is unnaturally still. She is completely unmoving, except the rise and fall of her chest. There's a mask strapped to her face, and an IV in her arm.

I give her hand a gentle shake. "Can you hear me? Can you respond?"

Nothing, not even a flutter of eyelids. *They're sedated.* Acidic bile starts to rise in my throat. I spin, and run to the bed across from hers, this one holding an olive-skinned woman with raven hair pooled under her head. I repeat my hand shaking routine, and touch her cheek softly, but still nothing. Making my way down the aisle, I spot a tablet attached to the foot of each bed. I pick one up, and see a medical file.

Anne Gray

Age: 24

Donor: 691205

16 weeks gestation

My eyes start to blur, and I'm unable to take in any more of the file. I look up and see through my angry tears that, sure enough, there is a small swell rising on this woman's stomach under her gown. I quickly scan the rest of the women in the room, and realize that over half of them have visibly swollen pregnant bellies.

The sound of a door opening pulls me from my sickened stupor. I spin, and let out a relieved breath to see it's Patrick.

"Sadie! You should have waited for me, what if someone had been in here!" he scolds me in a hushed tone. He glances to either side, and I see cold realization dawn on his face. "God in heaven, *no.*"

I turn, and continue walking toward the end of the aisle, checking each face. "Oh, Patrick!" I run past the next two beds when I see her.

She's there, in the last bed on the right. All the life and color gone from her face, she's as unnaturally still as the rest. The vibrant, spitfire, tornado of a woman reduced to a pale specter in a white gown, mask strapped to her face, IV in her left arm. *Josephine.*

Anger washes over me in a hot wave, and I grip her hand in mine tightly. "We're going to get you out of here, Jo. I swear it." I start looking for a way to unplug her, but Patrick stops me with a hand on my shoulder.

"Sadie, don't touch anything. She's been medically sedated. It could be dangerous to unhook any of this, when we don't know what they've given her."

"I can't leave her here, Patrick. I can't leave any of them." My voice goes shrill, even to my own ears, as anger and disgust battle inside me for supremacy.

A scuffling noise from the hall causes Patrick and me both to snap our heads up, to see Atlas and Nell running past the window. They spot us, and skid into the room with us.

Nell's first reaction is a sharp intake of breath, but Atlas surveys the room in silence. Nell runs over, spotting Josephine in the bed next to me.

"I think I'm going to be sick." She throws a hand over her mouth, and Patrick quickly grabs a small white trashcan and shoves it at her.

She turns and retches violently. I turn back to Josephine, and realize I'm squeezing her hand too hard. I force myself to loosen my grip, finger by finger.

Nell, done puking, runs a shaky hand over her mouth and dries her face with her sleeve. "What is this place?"

"I don't know, but we can't stay here," Atlas says coldly. "We found her, now we need to get out so we can do something about this before we're seen."

"Wait, look." Patrick points to a red, blinking light in the corner. "Do you think that's a camera?

Atlas's normally stoic expression turns dark in an instant. "We've got to find a way to wipe the feeds. You two stay here, we'll be back." The two of them race back into the hall, and out of sight past the window.

"How could they do this?" Nell's voice is shaking, and she's leaning against the foot of one of the beds across the aisle from Josephine. My eyes flit past her to land on the occupant of that bed. "Oh, no. It can't be—" I drop Josephine's hand back to her bed, and walk over to the rail-thin woman. Her once dark chocolate skin has taken on a pallor, but it's definitely her. *Aisha*. My hand flutters up to her cheek, no longer rounded and full of vitality.

"Do you know her, too?" Nell asks, sounding stronger by the minute.

My eyes burn with unshed tears as I answer, "Yes, her name is Aisha. I—I thought she was dead."

"She might rather be," Nell says darkly. I turn and see her inspecting the tablet with Aisha's medical information.

"Why, what does it say?"

"This is her fourth pregnancy in four years."

My eyes close of their own accord, my sadness like a suffocating blanket. "Lord, help us all."

The echo of running feet comes back down the hall, and Patrick and Atlas appear a second later.

Patrick flings open the door. "It's time to go. We disabled the cameras."

I slowly place Aisha's cool hand back on the bed, and I take in her sleeping face. "I won't forget you, Aisha. I will get you out of here, I promise."

The four of us file out of the room, back down the single hallway and turn toward the door. Atlas opens the door a crack, and peers out intently before swinging it all the way open.

"Quickly, straight to the ATVs. Heads down and stay as quiet as you can."

We run and hop onto them, and in under sixty seconds the men both have kick-started them, and we're headed for the tree line.

I shout so Patrick can hear me over the roar of the engines and crunching of the gravel path, "Why aren't we taking the trail?"

"There was a comm system in the office. The kidnappers have been dealt with and the guards are being sent back to their posts. We found the camera controls in a security office and wiped them, but that won't matter if they catch us right outside," he shouts back over his shoulder.

I tuck my head back against the back of his shirt, now stiff with dried sweat, and close my eyes. Images of sedated women roll across my vision, like butterflies pinned to a board for a grade-school science project. I open my eyes, ignoring the sting of the wind whipping my hair around my head in a thousand tiny stinging strands. The brush slides by, blending together in an earthy kaleidoscope of brown, green, and yellow.

How could this happen, and how are we going to stop it?

Fourteen

Aftermath

To my surprise, we ride our ATVs directly to the rocky outcropping behind our cottage. Patrick quickly hops off the ATV, rifle in hand, and scales the rocks. He disappears from sight for a moment before he returns without the rifle. Wordlessly, he climbs in front of me, and we head straight to the back entrance of the guest house. At some point while we were in the secret medical facility, the loud booms had stopped. Atlas dismounts and helps Nell off, and Patrick does the same before extending me his hand. I take it, fingers numb. Whether from the cold or shock, I can't tell.

On wooden legs, I climb the boardwalk steps after Nell, and follow her into the guest house. There's a hum of voices, but they wash over me, incomprehensible.

"Sadie, are you all right? Sadie?" Patrick's worried voice snaps me out of it. I look up from the floor, and lock eyes with his deep blue ones.

"No, I'm not. I may never be all right again." My voice sounds far away to my own ears.

"Sadie, I think you're in shock." He is holding me by both shoulders and gives me a small shake.

"I've got her, go get a cup of hot tea," Nell instructs him. She takes my hand and rubs my arm soothingly. "Come on, we're going to go sit over here."

She leads me to a blue striped couch, and I sit next to her. I try to focus on what's going on around me, but it's hard. My brain feels like it's stuck in a loop. I feel exhausted, even though it's probably barely past lunch time.

Patrick returns, and presses a mug of steaming tea into my hands. The warmth feels good against my chilled palms, so I take a sip. He stays there, crouched in front of me, until the mug is empty. At some point, the fog starts to clear. My gaze strays from my knees to Patrick's face, etched with concern.

"Hey there," he says soothingly. "Are you feeling a bit better? You had me worried." He touches my cheek, the brush soft and careful. I lean into his palm and close my eyes for a second. The vision of sedated women in white comes rushing back, and I snap them back open and lurch upright.

"Hey, it's okay. You're fine, we're fine." His voice is low, like he's talking to a spooked horse, and his hands are gentle on my forearms. "Nell, I'm going to go talk to the director about a new room. I'm not taking her back to that cottage. Will you stay with her until I get back?" Nell nods, and slips her arm around my shoulders after I settle back against the couch.

I lean into her, grateful for her support. Glancing over, I see that she's calm and collected, despite her initial reaction to the sight of the drugged women.

"How are you okay right now?" I ask, words barely above a whisper.

One side of her mouth quirks up in a sarcastic half-smile. "Believe it or not, that's not the first time I've hidden in a bathtub in fear for my life. My uncle is a mean drunk." She shrugs. "You adapt, or you die."

Her words slowly sink in, and the puzzle pieces fit themselves together in my head. Nell, scrawny, barely sixteen with nothing but a backpack at the shuttle station in Georada, and no family to see her off. Nell, flinching away from all human contact. Nell, unhappy to be matched with Atlas, a mountain of muscle. *She was running.*

"Does Atlas know?" I can't imagine him being happy that his wife has an abusive scumbag for a relative waiting back home.

A single, tight nod is her only response. We sit in silence until Patrick returns with a large, antique room key. He extends his hand for mine. "Come on, Sadie. They're putting us up in the guest house for a while."

I take his hand and stand, but turn back to Nell. "Thank you, Nell."

She smiles at me fondly. "No problem. Get some rest."

The next morning, I'm tired from a restless night's sleep, but feeling myself again otherwise. Patrick and I spent the rest of the day yesterday locked away in our new room. It's smaller than our cottage, but it has a balcony that looks over the dunes to the ocean. Each time I'd woken in the night with nightmares, he held me until I fell back asleep.

We make our way down for breakfast, and the ubiquitous pink-shirted waiter brings by a basket of pastries. I choose a cheese Danish, but only pick at it. My appetite hasn't been great. It doesn't feel right to be sitting around in a luxurious beach house, eating extravagant food while at least a dozen women are drugged and helpless a few miles away.

Before our breakfast arrives, Emmett and Carolina join us at our table.

"Good morning," Patrick greets them.

"Morning," Emmett says. His smile doesn't reach his eyes. After they've each selected a pastry, they clasp hands and look back at us. "We're leaving. We've put in a transfer request, and given the circumstances, they're letting us go today." The announcement is abrupt, but I'm not surprised.

"Where are you headed?" I ask.

"Playa Reino. We thought some distance and some sunshine would be a good change. I know you guys just got here, but I think they'd let you switch locations early given yesterday's—" Carolina's forehead wrinkles. "—*events.*"

Emmett shakes his head angrily. "How they expect to keep us in the dark when our safety is at stake, I'll never understand."

My eyebrows furrow. "What do you mean?"

"They won't tell us what the attack was about. Only that it was a group of extremists. Who is out there attacking honeymoon resorts? We deserve to know!" His fist slams the table, and I jump at the bang, still apprehensive after the latest attack.

Carolina puts her hand over his fist in a calming gesture. "Settle down, Emmett. We're leaving, that's all we can do."

Patrick's face is grim. "It was a kidnapping attempt," he announces, and Carolina's mouth falls open.

"Who were they trying to get?" Emmett asks, looking unsettled.

Patrick's gaze crashes into mine, before he looks back at Emmett and answers, "The women, most likely. There was a kidnapping attempt while we were at the NLC back in Georada. There are still extremist groups out there who think the world is better off without a large human population. When I was active in the guard, we got reports of cells they busted up, and experiments they were doing, trying to finish what the Sterilization Vector started so many years ago."

Carolina's grip tightens on Emmett's sleeve. "My word, are we safe anywhere?" she looks troubled.

"Anywhere is better than here, at this point," Emmett says darkly. "You should come with us."

Patrick and I exchange a glance. "I'm not going anywhere without Nell," I declare.

"Aww, I knew you liked me," Nell says as she saunters through the dining room door.

I snort, but don't disagree. Atlas speaks up. "Who's leaving?"

"We are. It's clearly not safe here anymore," Emmett answers.

Atlas nods. "It's probably for the best."

Breakfast is passed with minimal conversation, all centered around which parts of the NAA seem least likely to be the target of further kidnapping attempts. *Anywhere we aren't.* If the kidnappers are out to finish sterilizing humanity, my polymorph genes would be a huge prize.

As we finish up breakfast, another staff member brings a letter and hands it to Patrick. The handwriting matches his mother's. He opens it and scans the short missive with a tense expression before handing it to me.

Patrick,

Your security detail will arrive tomorrow. There's been another leak.

Stay Safe,

Deb

Frustration boils in my chest at the lack of detail. What kind of leak? Was that the kidnapping attempt, or is something else going to happen? My angry gaze lands on Patrick, who doesn't look any happier. Before anyone can question us, however, cha-cha music starts blaring from Patrick's pocket.

I groan as my wrist starts buzzing like an angry beehive is attached to it. The green band is lit up with two pink hearts. *Fertile week again.* After the alerts stop, Emmett and Carolina stand to leave.

"We probably won't see you again before we leave, since you'll be busy. But as soon as you're able, you should get out of here. Even if you don't join us in Playa Reino, get away from this place." Emmett shakes both of our hands, and Carolina hugs us.

"I guess we'd better head up," Patrick says, before handing the letter from his mother to Atlas. "Be on the lookout, please. We don't know what's coming."

Atlas scans it quickly, expression grim. "I think we'll see about getting a room down the hall."

I give them one last wave before we head up the stairs to our room.

Fertile week passes in a blur of old movies and room service meals. My favorite one is about a couple from the city who buy an old farm and become chicken farmers. We discovered that the TV works again after we track "activity" for the day. *Controlling jerks.* Something about the old, black-and-white simplicity lulls me to sleep at night. Patrick's warm arms and comforting masculine scent don't hurt, either.

After five days, though, we're both ready to get out of our room. Thankfully, the week was uneventful, and we didn't have any repercussions from our break-in at the medical facility, or the leak Deb warned us about. Whatever security detail they sent, they also didn't disturb us. We saw a black-clad man walking the beach a few times from our balcony, but other than that there's been no sign of security. However, now that we're allowed out of our room again, I'm sure we'll be meeting them. Patrick and I both have our tennis shoes on, and hope to get out on the walking trails with Atlas and Nell this morning to plan for our next steps. We've hashed out as many things as we can with the two of us, but we both agree we need Atlas's expertise on how to expose the evil that's going on here. One thing is for sure, we can't stay quiet and do nothing.

Fingers entwined, we walk down the stairs to the first floor of the guest house. At the bottom, a man with a broad back in a skin-tight camouflage t-shirt blocks our way. His chestnut hair is thick and shiny in the morning light streaming in from the many ocean-front windows. Our footsteps on the stairs must alert him to our descent because he turns, and my heart almost bursts out of my chest when I see his face.

"PETER!" I scream so loudly that Patrick jumps next to me, and I race down the last few stairs and fling myself right into my brother's waiting arms.

He hugs me tightly, lifting my feet right off the bottom stair step. "Hey, squirt, I hear you've been getting into trouble, as usual."

"I haven't done a thing," I scoff at his playful accusation. "I am a delight twenty-four-seven."

He laughs, loud and rambunctious. "I've missed you, Sadie. How are you? Is your new *husband* treating you well?" His annoyed emphasis on the word has me guiltily looking back to Patrick, who I'd abandoned without a second thought.

"I'm good, and yes. Peter, this is Patrick. Patrick, my middle brother Peter." I gesture between the two of them, and Patrick sticks his hand out to shake. Peter accepts, and a minor staring contest ensues. I wave both hands in front of them, breaking their focus on each other. "That's enough of that. Now, answer my question; why are you here? I thought you were on assignment on the west coast somewhere?" I link my arm through his on my left, and Patrick's on my right, and we walk to the dining room.

"I was, until I got Teddy's call. It took a lot of arm twisting, but I got reassigned. I'm part of your personal guard detail now." He levels me with a serious look. "So no more running off alone. If you're not in your room, me or one of the guys are with you, period."

"The guys? How many guys are we talking, exactly?" I squeeze Patrick's hand nervously.

"Me, plus three. You have four personal guards at all times, from here on out. As things progress and your new status becomes fully public, that will probably have to increase."

I swallow, making the logical leap. "So, I guess that means you know—" I trail off, unsure how to actually say it out loud. *Royalty.*

He nods. "Teddy was pretty hot under the collar about the whole situation when he called, and he gave me an earful. Don't worry, I talked him off the ledge." He levels a glare at Patrick. "You, however, are on his crap list."

Patrick looks contrite. "I don't blame him in the least. All I can do is try to make it up to him, at this point."

Peter stops at a breakfast table, and I let go of his arms to sit. Patrick sits next to me, and Peter pulls out the chair across from me. "So, if we have four guards, where are the other three?"

"Front door, back door, and off duty at the moment." He points to illustrate their locations.

"Well, we have a *lot* of catching up to do," I say, as the waiter arrives at our table.

We enjoy breakfast, just the three of us, and it's so nice to have a normal conversation for once. Another guard in camouflage approaches our table as we're finishing up.

"Peter, I'm here to relieve you." The man stands at attention, waiting for Peter's acknowledgement.

"I'm good for now, Spivey. Go tell Martinez to take his off shift." The man nods, spins on his heel, and leaves the dining room without comment.

"Now, do you two want to stay in the guest house? Because if not, they've prepared a new cabin for you. I understand your last one was damaged in the kidnapping attempt."

His words bring back the vivid image of the splintered bathroom door, and a pool of crimson staining the hallway. I shudder.

Patrick looks over at me. "It's up to you, Sadie. We'd have more space in the cottage, but if you feel safer in the guest house we can stay here."

"What are the four of you going to do, if we move back to a cottage?" I ask, and frown as I imagine them all standing around outside in the cold so I can have the illusion of privacy. Peter's silence is all the answer I need. "It's okay, we can stay in the guest house. That's probably easier, right?"

Peter nods, confirming my suspicions.

"Is that okay with you, Patrick?"

He squeezes my hand. "Just fine."

A crackle comes from Peter's comm wristband. "We've got a situation out front. Everyone report."

I exchange a worried glance with Patrick, as Peter surges to his feet. "You two stay here, I'll be right back."

I glance nervously at Patrick, but he looks unconcerned, as he sips his second cup of coffee. I see the guard who'd been dismissed for his rest come flying back down the stairs, and head in the same direction as Peter. A minute later, scuffling sounds come from the front door of the guest house, and I glance at Patrick again, my worry rising.

Still, he's calm as he sits there, drinking coffee like it's any other Tuesday. *I guess for him, it is just another Tuesday.*

Things quiet down, a door slams, and then Peter reappears. "Sorry about that, the media is getting bolder the longer they're out there."

I freeze to the spot. "What do you mean, the media? And how long have they been out there?"

He shrugs nonchalantly. "Ehh, five days? For the most part they stand in the driveway right past the grass hedge hoping for a shot of you two. Jokes on them because you've been locked in your room the whole time. Every now and then one of them makes a run for the front door, usually when one of the staff is carrying linens, or distracted on the phone. However, now that you two are out, I recommend a strict back-door policy for coming and going from the guest house."

He picks up his abandoned cup of coffee, and drains it in a single swallow, before taking in my pale face.

"It's okay, Sadie. The guys and I are on top of it. You're safe here." He shoots me a confident look, and I relax a hair. The idea of people standing outside, trying to photograph us is freaky, but I guess I need to get used to that.

An odd sound comes from the window to our left, and all of our heads whip over at the same instant. There, pressed against the window, is a short man in khaki cargo pants, with a camera in hand. He seems to recognize Peter, and then immediately lifts the camera and starts shooting right through the window.

Peter jumps into action like a shot, and darts straight to the back door of the guest house. The man lowers the camera, hits a few buttons, and then bolts. We watch in horrified fascination as Peter comes into view of the windows at a full run, another camouflaged guard we've not seen yet on his tail, and then hear a loud crash a few moments after they're out of sight.

A minute passes, and a smashing sound is the only noise from outside. Then Peter, walking now, comes back across the windows, a mangled black mess in his hand. He makes his way in and sits back down, plopping the now-destroyed camera on the table between us. Before I can say anything, a cheer erupts out front. Confused, I turn to Patrick.

He sighs, finally sets his coffee down on the table, and addresses Peter. "Well, the secret's out now. Auto-uploader?" He gestures to the smashed pile of technology in front of me.

What's an auto-uploader?

Peter's only response is a tight nod.

"What's an auto-uploader? You smashed the camera, so what's the issue?"

Peter points to a blue button before answering, "NAA One has equipped their best photographers with satellite-linked cameras. Every shot they take is uploaded directly to the media company's satellite as soon as they hit the button on the back. The signal isn't great here, but there's still a chance they got through before we smashed it. Even though the guy's going to jail for trespassing, they're all cheering because he got the shot. He's going to be wealthy when he gets out." Peter shakes his head, frustration clear.

"I'll make a call and see if they can do anything to stop it from seeing daylight," Patrick says calmly. He heads to the front, to make the call from the director's office. I, however, feel anything but calm.

FIFTEEN

ROYALLY SCREWED

O ur plans for a quiet day hiking and planning with Nell and Atlas are soured by the morning's run-in with the photographer. However, the urge to do something pushes me past my reluctance to run into any more khaki-clad nightmares. Once Atlas and Nell arrive to keep me company, Peter leaves to arrange the guards to ensure we don't have any repeat fiascos. The three of us are waiting for Patrick to return so we can make our exit.

"I can't believe somebody's willing to go to jail to get a picture of you. I mean, you're pretty and all, but not jail-worthy. No offense," Nell muses.

"I'm sure it was more the fat wad of money he's going to earn than my looks that encouraged him," I say drily.

"I don't know—I bet it would be big news if you were a hideous shrew. Patrick would be cast in a sympathetic light, doing his duty to further humanity, and the crown, despite your odiousness." Her dramatics know no ends.

Atlas puts a hand on her shoulder. "Nah, people are going to eat this up. Especially if word gets out about your high match rate or unique genetics."

My heart falls to my feet. "Oh, no. You don't think that's a possibility, do you? We aren't even supposed to know about that. How would the reporters get wind of it?"

He shrugs. "Same way Glitch did. Not to mention, there've been two leaks already. Somebody high up is benefitting from this information getting out, and pushing in the monarchy. From what Patrick has said, it's not his father. Most likely some well-connected lackey in the office, then, who stands to move up in the new order."

"I don't really care who it is; I don't want my family dragged into this. If word gets out about me being *different*, they'll all get dragged through the wringer with me." I drop my face into my hands. I hadn't thought about the multi-layered crap storm that would ensue if my new political position came head to head with my genetic anomaly.

Can't anything go right? How are we supposed to free those women with a security detail, media hounding us, and the Damocles's sword of my genetics?

Patrick walks back in, and I can tell right away that he's angry. He strides over to where the three of us wait, and runs his hands through his hair. "Let's get out of here. I have a lot to tell you," he says as he meets my eyes. "All of you."

It takes finagling, but eventually it's agreed that the four of us, plus Peter and one other guard, are enough to go out on the beach. We brave the buffeting ocean wind, rather than the more protected hiking trails, so that we're less likely to be overheard by our guard detail.

"So, our lives just got a lot more interesting," Nell observes, once we're spread out. Peter trails behind us at a distance, and the other guard, Rolf, is about 30 yards ahead. "How are we supposed to get anything done now?"

"My thoughts exactly," I agree.

"It's about to get worse," Patrick says, his disgruntled voice is barely above a mumble. "I spoke with my mother. The photographer this morning got three shots uploaded before the camera stopped transmitting. So, now, they know where we are, who we are, and what we look like." He stops talking, and that sinks in for a moment.

"So, what happens now? There's no way to get NAA One not to run it? Your father's the prime minister; won't they do him a favor to protect your privacy?" Nell asks.

His face turns thunderous. "Mom informed me that they're choosing instead to get ahead of it. Candy Thomas from NAA One will be here, with a full film crew—tomorrow—to interview us for the national news." He looks at me apologetically. "Apparently we're about to make our public debut as a couple." His mouth flattens into a thin line of displeasure.

"So, that's it, then? Our cover is blown, everyone is going to know where we are, and we've already got paparazzi stalking us at the guest house," I say, still trying to fully grasp the change that's happening in my life.

"Unfortunately, that about sums it up." I can hear the simmering anger in his voice.

"But how are we supposed to help those women if we've got people watching our every move?" Nell's question is the same one I've been turning over myself, ever since the beginning. *Where do we go from here?*

"We don't," Atlas answers.

"There's *no way* we're leaving them there and forgetting about it!" Nell's reaction is instant, and heated.

"Didn't say we were. But we can't do jack with a twenty-four-seven guard, paparazzi stalking the front gate, and no proof." His rebuttal quiets us all.

"What do you recommend, Atlas? Even as the prime minister's son, I can't haul out an accusation of this magnitude with no proof. It would be too easy for whoever's running things to make them all disappear. And if they're willing to drug and impregnate unwilling women, I can imagine what they'd do with them if they knew they'd been caught," Patrick says.

I shudder, the implication chilling me worse than the cutting wind off the ocean.

"We have to get out of here."

"That's what I was afraid you were going to say." Patrick lets out a gusty sigh.

I push my windswept hair back from my face. "How is leaving going to help? Going to another resort is only going to draw the media attention there, and the guards."

"That's why we can't go to another resort. We've got to get out of the system. Otherwise, we're sitting ducks to be snatched ourselves."

His words echo the fears I've been holding onto ever since they dragged Josephine away. "What's the alternative? If we leave, we'll be putting a target on our backs." I point out.

"Leave the escape plans to me," Atlas says, "I've got an idea how we might be able to pull it off in a way that we're not incriminated for escaping, but I'll have to call in a few favors. The question is, how do we get the proof?" he says cryptically.

"I actually had an idea about the proof. Glitch is still around, right Patrick?" I ask.

He nods. "He's just laying low in the next town over, why?"

"Well, you guys found the security camera setup in that facility. What if Glitch could hack into it, record the women in there? Once we had video proof, maybe even video of whoever is guarding and caring for them, we would have something to use to show your father, or whoever needs to see it to stop it," I suggest.

Atlas is the first to respond. "It could work. Do you think Glitch could hack it? We have no idea what network the footage is on, or what kind of security protocol they're typically running inside."

"All we can do is ask. I'm sure he's up for the challenge."

Later that evening, a brisk knock sounds on our guest room door. We'd been snuggling on the couch, watching an action movie Patrick picked this time. He gets up, taking his warm shoulder with him, and answers the door.

A tanned, leggy brunette in a pink dress that barely hits her mid-thigh is on the other side. Her brunette hair is pulled tightly back into a French twist, not a strand out of place. "Hello, I'm Brooke," she says, taking Patrick in from head to toe.

I bristle at her blatant perusal of my husband and stand from the couch. A second later, I remember that I'm wearing the dreaded bow-covered pajamas and pull at the hem in regret at their wrinkled state. *Them being less wrinkled won't make them any less embarrassing to be seen in. Ugh.* I'd considered getting rid of them, but my first kiss with Patrick happened in these pajamas. They're with me for life, now.

"Hello, Brooke, can I help you?" he says politely. To his credit, his eyes don't stray to the impressive display of tanned legs. I can barely look away, myself; she's nearly a foot taller than me.

She gives him a flirtatious smile that makes me want to bite my own tongue off. "Yes, I'm here to see about your wardrobe for tomorrow's interview. Well, both of your wardrobes," Brooke amends, once she finally notices me standing behind Patrick. "Your mother sent me."

"Ahh. Well, come on in, I guess." Patrick looks over his shoulder and shoots me an apologetic grimace.

"Delightful." She turns and pulls a rack I hadn't noticed crammed full of clothes in behind her. "Wow, not much room to maneuver in here," she observes as Patrick barely manages to scrape the door shut behind the rack. "You'd think being royalty would get you a bit more space."

"We're not royalty yet," I remind her. "The coronation is still a month away."

She waves a hand at me in dismissal. "Details, minor details. For all intents and purposes, you're royal. Not very tall, but royal." She scrunches her nose as she scrutinizes me.

How rude can you be? I think angrily. But I keep it to myself, my mom's voice echoing in my ears so many times over the years to "be kind, or be quiet." I thought that advice would get easier as I aged, but *boy*, was I wrong.

Brooke claps twice, snapping me away from my thoughts of my mom. "Okay, now that I've seen you both, it's time to get down to business. Patrick, they want you in a suit. Sadie, they want you in a dress. I've got a variety of cuts here, but a few of these are going to be long . . . unless you're comfortable in a pair of high heels?" She rummages in the bottom basket of the rolling rack and comes up with a pair of white platform stilettos at least four inches high.

"Uh, not so much. I usually wear tennis shoes or cowboy boots."

Her hand flies to her chest, and from the look on her face you'd think I kicked her dog. "Well"—she sniffs —"that will be the *first* thing we work on. A princess, even by marriage, can't very well go around in cowboy boots." She spins back to the rack and starts tossing clothes onto our bed, so she misses the angry glare I direct at Patrick.

Sorry he mouths at me.

"Patrick, you're up first. Be a dear and go pop these on so I can see how they fit." She hands him a hanger with a blue suit, and a honeyed smile.

He walks slowly to the bathroom, and gives me one last apologetic look before he shuts the door, leaving me alone with Brooke-the-fashion-Amazonian. Her focus narrows on me as soon as the door clicks shut behind him, and I barely stop myself from taking an involuntary step back.

What is it about overly-coiffed women that always makes me uncomfortable?

She shoves a white gown towards me. "Try this on first. It will probably be too long, but hopefully not by as much as the others.

I accept the dress, but look around awkwardly and realize there's nowhere to change. She rolls her eyes at my hesitation. "Go on, I'll turn around. Although I must tell you, I've seen it all before."

True to her word, she spins and faces the bathroom door, arms crossed across her chest. Quickly shucking off my childish pajamas, I slip the dress over my head. It has a plunging neckline, and a gather on one side over halfway up my thigh. I'm trying to arrange it to cover more of my cleavage when she tuts, and I look up to see her inspecting me again. "No, that's not what we're looking for at all. Too sexy." She flips through the rack again, and hands me another dress, also white.

I toss the first dress on the bed and pull on the next one. Thankfully the zipper is on the side, and it zips in one fluid motion. I look down and take in the one-shoulder, fitted gown. It's pretty, but not at all my style. There is a large fabric ruffle on the side with the shoulder, and the other side swoops daringly low.

The bathroom door opens, and Patrick re-enters looking hot as Hades in the blue suit. His white dress shirt has one button undone at the top, and my eyes are immediately drawn to the tiny snippet of skin I can see there.

"Oh dear, that's all wrong. We don't want you looking like some old presidential candidate. That's so last century." She shudders, and hands him a different suit before shooing him back to the bathroom. She turns to me, and looks exasperated. "That won't work, either. They didn't tell me you had so much cleavage." The glare she gives me implies I somehow had control over this, which I would like to assure her, *I did not.*

She taps her chin and assesses me with a frown. "I think I have *one* gown which might work. To think, I almost didn't bring it because it's the wrong color."

She hands me a third gown, and I wait for her to turn back around before stripping again. This one slides over me in a smooth rush of deep blue gossamer silk. It settles, right at my toes, and the split sleeves allow for plenty of freedom of movement for my arms. It almost looks Greek, like a goddess's robes from the stories I read growing up. The neckline is high, and the gathered material hugs my collarbone. The only risqué bit is that the waist is made with see-through lace, with gold threaded details stitched throughout and my bare skin showing underneath. Of the three options, it still leaves the most to the imagination.

"Ah, yes. That's much better. I think we have a winner." She claps once, and gestures for me to hand it back to her. Before I do, the bathroom door opens again and Patrick steps out in a silvery pin-striped suit. It fits him like a glove, and he looks mouth-wateringly good.

His eyes, however, lock on me in the Grecian gown. "Wow, you look gorgeous." He peruses me from the pooled hem up to my messy, bed head.

I blush. "You look quite dashing, yourself."

"Aww, newlyweds. All blushes and romantic fluttering eyelashes. They were right to choose white, but royal blue makes a powerful statement of its own." Brooke gestures for us to hand the clothes back, so Patrick retreats back into the bathroom. He tosses one more heated look at me before shutting the door.

"Why are all the other dresses white, now that you mention it?" The question comes out muffled, as I pull the dress over my head.

"Oh, you know, that's the image they want to portray for the public's first time seeing you. White is innocent, virginal, pure, all the good stuff." She waves, as if it's of no import.

Sacrificial lambs are white, also. I sigh and pull the infamous bow pajamas back on over my messy hair. Quite a few tendrils have escaped my nightly ponytail, and I feel like a disheveled child next to the statuesque beauty with the tailored designer clothes.

Patrick emerges, and hands the suit back to Brooke. How does he still look so good in his lounge clothes? His t-shirt and soft pajama pants cling slightly to his defined chest and trim waist, and his hair is perfectly swooped to one side. He looks like a god, even at eleven p.m.. Life isn't fair.

Brooke, satisfied with our clothing choices, promises to have them steamed and ready to go for the interview tomorrow morning before pushing the overstuffed rack back into the hallway. One of the guards—Spivey, I think—is waiting to carry it back down the stairs for her.

Patrick shuts and locks the door, before turning and striding across the room to me. He reaches both hands around and presses them to my lower back, fingers playing with the hem of my pajama top.

"You," he says, and kisses me on the nose—"were an absolute vision"—another kiss, this time to the cheek—"in that dress." He kisses the other cheek. "If Brooke hadn't been here, I'd have *loved*"—this time the kiss lands just below my earlobe—"to help you out of it."

I shudder at the promise in his words, yet still can't help but ask, "You weren't too distracted by brunette Barbie?"

He chortles low in his throat, the vibration traveling through his lips to my jaw, where he's kissing now. "Brunette Barbie doesn't stand a chance against my little spitfire." He kisses along my jawline, leaving a delicious trail of sparks in his wake, and suddenly I forget to be worried about anyone's opinion except his.

The next morning dawns, and my least favorite chimes in the world wake me when the sun is barely over the balcony railing.

I pull my pillow over my head, fully intending to ignore the cursed thing, until Patrick rubs my shoulder. "Hon, I'm sorry, but you have to get up. The beauty crew are already waiting downstairs."

"No," I groan, "it's too early. We didn't get nearly enough sleep last night."

He chuckles. "Funny, I didn't hear any complaints at the time."

I decide my pillow makes a much better weapon than it does a barrier, and whack him with it. He laughs and steps out of swinging range. "Come on, I'll run down and get you some cocoa." He peppers kisses across my nose, and I give him a tiny smile in return. *He is impossible to stay annoyed with.*

True to his word, he heads out of our room, and I flop back against the bed, in no hurry to get up and start getting made up for this interview. The interview that's going to be on *national television.* I lay there for a few minutes, dreading having the perky newscaster question us, until I sit bolt upright in the bed as a thought hits me—*my parents are going to see this interview!*

At the same moment, Patrick backs in through our door while balancing two mugs.

"Patrick, we have a problem." I try not to sound panicked, but nonetheless, he turns too quickly, and sloshes hot coffee on his wrist.

"Shoot! Ahh, that stings!" He quickly sets the cups down, and sits on the edge of the bed, which I still haven't left. "What's wrong?"

"I have to talk to my parents!"

He looks confused. "Uhm, okay, but you know that they don't really allow any outside communications except in case of emergencies, right? Even letters are screened, and they don't give us much mail."

I shake my head. "This is an emergency! My parents are going to see this interview today. See me sitting next to you, being called the future *Princess* of the NAA, and they have no clue. I have to call them, Patrick. I don't know if Teddy's told them, or what he's told them!"

He grabs both of my hands, which had been flapping eccentrically, and holds them between his larger ones. "Okay, I'll talk to the director. It's not usually allowed, but they let me put in a call to my mother yesterday, given the circumstances. Although, while I hate to say it, you probably shouldn't tell them *too much*, in case the line is recorded."

I nod. "That makes sense. I just can't let them get blindsided by this. I'm sure Teddy's told them something, but they deserve to hear it from me, not a news anchor."

"I agree, hearing it from you would be best. You'd better get moving then! We'll try to get you a phone call first, but you're already late for your makeup."

"Okay, okay! I'm going now!" I fly out of bed, with new motivation propelling me.

I rush through my usual morning routine, throw my hair in a bun—ignoring all of the wispy fly-aways, as usual—and in record time, I'm taking Patrick's hand and heading down the stairs.

The main floor of the guest house has been overrun with people. Cameras, equipment, lights, and people wearing various headsets clog up the usually empty area, and I stop in my tracks.

"Are these people all here for us?" I whisper, leaning closer to Patrick on reflex.

"Yep, sure are. Let's scoot past and go see the director first." He leads me straight to an office nestled off the front entrance of the resort and knocks on the closed door.

A moment later, Jared opens the door and gestures us inside. "How can I help you this morning?" he asks, settling behind his ornate mahogany desk.

"I need to make a phone call. My parents don't know about all of this, and I don't want them to hear about it on the evening news." I gesture at the doorway, where sounds of the unusual crowd of people are filtering into his office.

He steeples his fingers together, considering my request. "As I told you yesterday, we have a very strict policy regarding outside contact. We allow some letters, but otherwise we feel that it's best if your focus remains here, on the new family you're building, rather than outside, with the people waiting for you." He stops and gives us a very stern look.

That wasn't a no. I simply stare back, waiting him out.

After a lengthy pause, he finally sighs in surrender. "All right, given the unusual circumstances, we'll allow it. Only this once, and please do not tell anyone else that you were able to call home. This really can't become a regular occurrence." This, he directs at Patrick with a testy squint.

"Thank you so much for understanding! We won't abuse it; I can't let my parents hear this news from a stranger on television."

He nods, hands me a sleek silver phone, and heads for the door. At the last second he pauses, hand on the knob. "I'll be back in five minutes." Then slips out, and the door shuts behind him with a soft click.

Who to call? I dial my mom first, and the phone disappointingly rings through to her voicemail. She's probably not going to answer, since she doesn't know it's me. "Mom, it's Sadie. I have some news I wanted to tell you myself before you hear it elsewhere. I only have access to this phone for five minutes, please call me back! I'm going to call Dad next. Love you, bye!" I quickly hang up, and dial my father.

Thankfully, he picks up on the second ring. "Hello," the sound of his voice, exactly how I remember it, chokes me up so much that I forget to respond at first. "Hello?" he says again, and I finally remember to speak.

"Dad! It's Sadie! I've missed you so much." My voice comes out scratchy around the building tears.

"Sadie! Oh, baby, it's so good to hear your voice. Is everything okay?" There's a shuffling sound, and then he hollers, "Marie! Sadie's on the phone, get in here."

I can hear my mother's voice from a distance. "Sadie? I thought she wasn't allowed to call! Wait, why did she call you, instead of me?"

"I don't know yet! Sadie, are you still there?"

"Yes, Dad, I'm here. I'm so glad you're both there. I need to tell you something, and I only have a few minutes." I have to smile at their usual back and forth, and Patrick squeezes my hand.

"Hang on, I'll put you on speaker." I hear a beep, and he continues, "Okay, Sadie, what do you need to tell us?"

"Well, I—" I trail off, unsure of how to start, but the time crunch doesn't allow me to overthink it. "I'm going to be on the news this afternoon. I wanted you to know, beforehand, so you wouldn't be surprised." I pause, but they stay quiet. "I'm actually here now with my new husband, Patrick. He's—he's really amazing, and I think you guys are going to love him." I pause again, looking over at Patrick, who gives me an encouraging nod.

"But here's the thing, and I don't know what Teddy may have already told you, but, well, he's Patrick Royce. The prime minister's son." My dad blows out a breath, but otherwise stays silent. I close my eyes. "I needed you to hear that from me. Before you see me in a news interview. He's not who I expected to get matched with, but he's a really great person. And I hope you guys will give him a chance, and love him too, in time. That's all—" I stop, the lump in my throat preventing further rambling.

"Baby, if he makes you happy, he could be from Mars for all we care. You sound happy, sugar. Are you? Does he make you happy?"

"Yeah, Daddy, he does." My voice is small, and Patrick squeezes my hand again in support.

"Then that's all that matters. It's going to be fine, baby." His voice is so reassuring, I feel a tear leak from the corner of my eyes.

"I wish I could have told you in person, but I'm afraid this is the best I can do. I would give anything to hug you both right now. Hopefully soon." I try not to let them hear the sadness rolling through me, and soak in their voices like a desert soaks up rain.

"Oh, sweetie, we miss you more than anything! But you'll be home soon, and things can start getting back to normal. Just like Teddy and Faith!" my mom says with happiness.

"How are Teddy and Faith? Are they doing okay?" I ask, glad for the temporary change of focus.

"Oh, they're great! Faith is absolutely lovely. She's been a little sick, but don't you worry—I'm taking good care of her. We couldn't have asked for a sweeter daughter-in-law." My mom's gushing tone tells me all I need to know. *No way is Faith leaving for New Texas when her three years is up. She's one of us now.* That happy thought bolsters me.

"Can I speak with them for a moment?" Patrick asks quietly from my side.

"Sure! Hey, Mom and Dad? Patrick wants to say hello." I push the button to put the phone on speaker.

"Hello, Mr. and Mrs. Taylor?" he says, his voice a hint lower than usual.

"Hello, son," Dad says.

"I'm sorry that we aren't able to meet in person, but I wanted to let you both know that I love your daughter dearly, and I intend to do everything in my power to make her happy. I know our situation is a bit *different* than many, but, I love her—with all of my heart. I thought you should know that."

It's silent for a beat, and then I hear my mom sniffle. "Thank you for speaking with us, Patrick. It's good to hear that you two have made a real match."

The office door behind us opens a crack. "Time's up," Jared says, but he doesn't open the door the rest of the way.

The rock in the pit of my stomach returns. "We have to go. I love you both so, so much. Watch the news later! Tell everyone we said hello!"

"Bye, honey!" They both say their farewells, and I end the call with a pang of regret.

Jared walks back in. "I assume everything is in order now?"

I nod, and swipe furiously at a tear that's rolling down my cheek.

"Yes, thank you," Patrick says, courteous when I'm unable to speak.

"Very good. I believe your captive audience awaits." he gestures to the door with a grimace. We stand, and Patrick puts his arm around my waist, and gives me a minute to scrub the last trace of tears from my cheeks before pulling open the door.

Here goes nothing.

Sixteen
EYE CANDY

Hair and makeup for TV are quite a process. The two men who did it, Giles and Chris, were like a tornado of constant motion and swirling instruments. They circled me non-stop for nearly an hour, chastising me the first half for not giving them enough time to "perfect their canvas," which apparently, is me. Brooke showed up too, the royal Grecian dress in tow. By the time they were done with me, I felt like an ancient sacrifice, ready to be tossed into the volcano to appease the fertility gods.

"Honey, you have got to stop frowning like that. We have done our part to make you into an ethereal goddess of the modern ages, but if you keep scowling you're going to age before your time and look ugly on a postage stamp. Is that what you want?" Giles pauses for a split second. "No, I didn't think so. Now, don't waste my glamour on frown lines. Smile, and lift your chin. You're about to become a princess among mere mortals; you need to act the part." He puts two fingers under my chin, and lifts it until I notice the handheld mirror he's offering me.

I take it, afraid to see if I look like a clown, as long as they've been painting and plucking me. I drink in my reflection with a quiet gasp. Not a clown. They've instead polished me so that I now shine like a jewel. I'm still me, of course—brunette, freckles, blue eyes. The summer glow of ranch work has started to fade from my skin, but they've got it radiating a cool vitality.

"Wow," is all I manage.

"*Wow*, she says. That's it? We've turned you into a princess masterpiece worthy of an epic ballad, and all we get is *wow*?" Chris snorts. "We've got our work cut out with this one, Brookie."

Brooke shakes her head but doesn't comment. She already made her disdain for me clear, when I refused to wear the shiny white patent-leather platform heels *again* this morning. She finally produced a simple gold bootie with delicate embossed leather, which I happily donned. *I am so not giving these shoes back.*

"Do you like your hair, sweetie?" Giles reaches up and gestures to where my brunette tresses have been twisted into the most intricate braided crown I've ever seen. He's even tucked tiny iridescent crystals into the strands, so that I sparkle with every turn.

"It's gorgeous, you've really outdone yourselves," I say, giving him an appreciative smile. "It kind of looks like I'm wearing a crown," I observe, tentatively touching one of the loops with a hidden gem.

He chuckles and softly swats my hand away from his masterpiece. "That's the idea, sweetie. You only get one chance to make a first impression. Your debut has to scream royalty, down to the last detail."

"Well, it definitely looks . . . royal," I agree.

A soft knock at the door grabs all of our attention, and a moment later Patrick enters, stunning in the pin-striped suit. Brooke saunters across the room to him.

"Patrick, darling," she simpers, making my skin crawl and my hackles rise as she lays a hand on his chest. "I've got one final touch for you."

He gives her a tight smile and removes her hand. His gaze scans the room and quickly lands on me, still seated in the spinning barber's chair. His eyes turn to molten heat in the way I've come to love.

"You look absolutely stunning," he says, and his eyes travel from my braided crown slowly down to the tips of my golden-booted-toes. Heat suffuses me at his obvious perusal, and I blush.

"Whoo, child, is it hot in here or is it just me?" Giles fans his face with an exaggerated gesture, eyes locked on Patrick.

"Patrick, I've got your pocket square," Brooke snaps, clearly unhappy with his lack of receptiveness to her overly friendly greeting.

That's right, Brookie. He's not interested. My possessiveness surprises me, but her blatant interest in Patrick is grating on my nerves.

He turns back to her and allows her to arrange a rich purple satin square into the tiny pocket on his suit jacket. It's the only pop of color, as he has no tie, and his top shirt button is undone and draws my eye like a magnet.

Once she's perfected its position, she claps her hands together briskly, all business now that she's been rebuffed. "It's time, lovebirds. Candy should be here any minute to start your interview."

Candy Thomas, the perky blonde news anchor for NAA One. *Oh boy.*

Patrick slips his arm around my waist, and the contact bolsters me.

He leads me out of the room we'd taken over for interview preparations, and down the short hall to the conference room. The bustle of people is still there, but it's quieter. Like someone has pulled a wool blanket over the area, stifling the energy from earlier.

The first person turns and sees us approaching, and whips around with his camera. His motion sparks a domino effect, and suddenly the quiet hum is a buzz of anticipation.

"Right this way, Mr. and Mrs. Royce!" The first man gestures into the conference room, which is glowing, even in broad daylight, with the number of portable lights they've set up.

Patrick gives him a nod, but I'm too busy trying to hold down my breakfast as my nerves spike. I have no desire to be on television, whatsoever. The idea of nearly every person in the entire NAA seeing this later is alarming. There's only one news station left, so every citizen except the most rural will likely see this within the next twenty-four hours. I swallow, regretting my choice of pastries and hot cocoa for breakfast.

Gripping Patrick's hand tightly in mine, we are greeted by the tan, intimidatingly tall Candy Thomas. Her smile is wide, and in the excessively-lit room, near-blinding.

"Well, lovebirds, nice of you both to join us!" she says by way of introduction. "Everyone is so thrilled to get a peak at the newlyweds, we almost couldn't take the anticipation!" She looks us both up and down, before offering a hand to Patrick, and then me, to shake.

Her grip is cool, and light on mine. "Nice to meet you," I say, and my voice cracks at the end.

She grimaces, and snaps her fingers at the crowd hovering behind us in the doorway. "Get the girl some water, would you? And give us a little space. She's a nervous wreck." She gestures vaguely in my direction, and the crowd moves back a few steps before she turns her eagle eye back to us.

"Now, if you two would have a seat, we can go ahead and get started once you've had a sip of water."

A young man in cargo pants comes running into the room with a glass of water. He stops a few feet away from our position on the loveseat, as if he's scared to come any closer.

Candy rolls her eyes. "They won't bite you. Now hurry up, we're behind schedule." She snaps again, and the man hands me the water before quickly scurrying back out the door.

"Thank you!" I call to his retreating back, but he doesn't acknowledge me.

"So, this is going to be a pretty light piece. I know you're new to the camera, so try to focus on me and pretend it's simply the three of us having a nice Sunday afternoon chat in your living room. It's not live, so it can be edited if need be. The prime minister's office requested a get-to-know-you, with a few details about where you're from, your home life, how you're liking the resort, and so on. Nothing earth-shattering, so no need to be nervous."

She smiles again, and I envy her ease in the middle of the chaotic atmosphere. After taking a few sips of my water, Candy gestures and another aid bustles in to take it away. Two cameramen file in, and post themselves in either corner of the room. One of them nods to Candy and a red light appears on the camera.

"Good Evening, citizens of the North American Alliance! Candy Thomas here, with an exclusive interview. I am thrilled to be the first to introduce you to none other than Patrick and Sadie Royce, the son and daughter-in-law of Prime Minister Royce." She lifts her thin arm in an elegant gesture and the cameras sweep toward us. I force a smile, and will my brain to slow down and focus.

Patrick lifts his hand in a small wave, so I follow suit.

"Patrick, how does it feel to finally, after all these years, be open about your identity?"

One side of his mouth lifts, a sardonic smile briefly appearing before he answers, "Well, it is definitely a change to have cameramen camped outside. But, it comes with the territory."

"Yes, we've all seen the photographs taken of you two, enjoying your breakfast earlier this week. That must have been a shocking moment, when the two of you have been trying to focus on building a new family." She pauses, and we both nod. "How is that going, by the way? Have you two enjoyed your time here at the honeymoon resort?" She raises her eyebrows expectantly.

Sure, except the part with the secret medical facility full of sedated women, and the mandatory sex tracking. I keep my sarcasm to myself.

"Mairmont is lovely, we've really enjoyed taking in the fall foliage, as well as the beaches and the local landmarks," I say instead.

Candy jumps at the chance to dig deeper. "Ahh, an outdoors enthusiast! Tell me, Sadie, did you spend a lot of time outdoors back home?"

I nod. "Yes, my family owns a ranch down south. We all work the herds together."

"All? How many family members do you have?" She waits expectantly, and I force myself to ignore the pit in my stomach.

"Well, my parents, my brothers and I, plus my sisters-in-law and two nephews." I try to gloss over the fine details.

"It must be nice to live so close to family," she says, and her warmth seems genuine. I allow myself to relax a hair.

"Patrick, how do you feel about having been matched with a wife with such a strong family waiting for her at home?"

"Sadie is such an amazing woman, there is no way her family could be anything less. I'm happy she has that support system in her life, for whenever our family starts growing." He gives my hand a gentle squeeze.

Candy presses a hand to her heart. "Oh my, you heard it here first! Patrick Royce, already planning a family with Sadie. I have to say, the attraction between the two of you is clear."

I duck my head, embarrassed with the abrupt turn in the conversation.

Patrick slips an arm around my shoulders, as if it can protect me from the prying Candy. "We've been very blessed, that our genetic match turned out to be a love match, too."

Candy leans forward, eyes gleaming with intent. "Sadie, some would say you've been the most blessed of all. Here you are, an average girl from a ranching family, and you win the genetic lottery and are matched with the single most eligible man on the entire continent. How do you feel about the fact that so many women would kill to be in your shoes right now?"

My brain spins, trying to think of an appropriate diplomatic answer. "I can see why people might think they'd want to be in my shoes, but Patrick's family responsibility is not something either of us takes lightly."

"That's understandable, given the weight on your shoulders. After all, you're about to be made royalty! The two of you, and your future son or daughter will rule one of the largest nations in the modern world." She pauses for dramatic effect. "Speaking of future children, any news you'd like to share today?"

It is not okay to punch someone on national television. It is not okay to punch someone on national television. I'm too busy repeating my new mantra to answer, so Patrick slides in smoothly.

"Not at this time. As you know, even with the NLC's genetic matching technology, it is not a quick or guaranteed process."

A mask of sympathy falls across her features. "Yes, it's so true. The heartbreak of childlessness is still far from eradicated. What would you say to the citizens out there dealing with this same situation, or those soon to be pulled into the Compulsory Marriage Program?"

It's my turn to jump in. "I would say that your ability to bear children doesn't define your worth as a person. You're not alone, and there is hope. There is *always* hope." I repeat it, hoping that it sinks in for me, as well as anyone watching. *We have to have hope.*

"What a touching sentiment, Sadie. Thank you for sharing that. Now, I have one final question for you, before we let you two get back to your honeymoon." She pauses, and locks her eyes on the camera lens, as if sharing a secret with the viewers. When she turns back to us, something about her mischievous smile gives me a bad feeling in the pit of my stomach.

"We have received information from an anonymous source that you two are an *exceptionally* high match." She takes another dramatic pause and stares conspiratorially into the camera lens. "So high, in fact, that it's the highest recorded match in the history of the NLC program. We know you two have been here going on a few months now, so, we have to ask —how do you feel about the fact that your brother and his wife have already conceived, and you two are still here, stuck waiting? You two are responsible for the continuation of the *royal* line, after all—that must add an enormous amount of pressure."

My jaw drops at her audacity at dragging my family into this, and then trying to pit us in some twisted competition, on top of that. Anger starts to bubble like lava inside of me, but I force the serene smile back into place on my face. I lock eyes with Candy and her smirk nearly pushes me right over the edge.

Patrick must have felt the change in my demeanor, because he gives a barely perceptible squeeze with his arm that's still wrapped around my shoulders.

"Oh, Candy," I say, my most charming southern twang underlaid with steely intent. "I'm afraid I'll have to disappoint you on this one. You see, I'm old-fashioned. Whenever our families have such good news, we celebrate with them. Life is not a competition, and the only thing I feel towards my brother is pride and joy. I'm sure you can understand. Now"—I stand gracefully, thankful for my foresight in refusing to wear the awful platform shoes—"if you'll excuse us, we do have to be going."

Patrick stands tall at my side, gives Candy a firm nod, and we exit the room hand-in-hand without looking back. The sea of recording personnel parts to allow our escape, a few of them gaping at our unscheduled exit.

Too dang bad, I think angrily, but keep the tepid smile fixed on my face. We reach the stairs, and I fly up them ahead of Patrick, and quickly shove my way into our room, and straight out the glass door onto our balcony. The sounds of the ocean wash over me. Eyes closed, cold wind whipping my carefully-pinned hair. Patrick joins me, but doesn't say anything, letting me have my moment of solitude. Once my face is numb and my arms are covered in chill bumps, I finally open my eyes. Patrick is observing me intently from the rocking chair.

"I'm sorry. I know it's unprofessional to leave an interview early, and I'm sure they're going to have a field day with that answer, but, it's none of her business, *anyone's* business if I'm pregnant or not. Who is she to put that expectation on us? Do people not realize that some women go their entire life and never have a full-term pregnancy?" I start to pace the length of the small balcony. "Patrick, this could all be moot for me. You will be prince, sure. But under the current laws, if I don't get pregnant in the next three years, I won't stay the princess, you'll be married off to the next best genetic match and she'll be the one by your side through the rest of this . . . whatever happens next." I gesture vaguely into the distance.

He finally stands, and steps into my path, forcing me to stop and look up at him. "Don't apologize. I think you were amazing, especially for your first ever interview. And, Sadie, you and I both know that's not going to happen." His voice is calm, certain.

"No, we don't, Patrick. We don't know anything. We *hope* it's not going to happen; we hope things will work between us, but . . . there are no guarantees anymore. The best science we have still isn't a sure thing." He rubs his hands up and down my chilled arms for a moment, before he shucks his suit jacket and wraps it around me. The warmth and his familiar masculine scent roll over me in a wave of comfort, and I shudder. He then cups my cheeks in his warm hands, making me feel sheltered.

"You're right, Sadie. We don't know for certain that we'll be able to have kids. But, can you honestly tell me that you think in three years things will be the same as they are now? That we'll have to get divorced? Because I don't. With what we know, what we have to uncover . . ." He pauses, shaking his head. "It's going to be a different world by then. It has to be."

At his words, an entirely different responsibility weighs heavily on my shoulders. The worry about being separated from Patrick still dogs my thoughts . . . But he's right. If it's not different by then, it means we've failed to expose the corruption and lies—and that's unacceptable.

SEVENTEEN

THE GIRL OUT OF THE COUNTRY

A nother day dawns, and I awake warm and snuggled into Patrick's arms. Every new day waking up in the same way is a kind of torture. In a way, this is our honeymoon, and we're happy together in our secluded bubble. But the pristine solitude hides a seething underbelly of corruption, and I can't truly enjoy our luxurious surroundings, knowing what's hidden in the woods a short distance away.

I sneak to the bathroom to take care of my urgent need to pee, and spot the little stack of urine collection cups that were delivered last night.

Ugh, testing time again already. At least I won't have to go far to drop it off now that we're in the guest house.

I grab a cup, collect a urine sample, and wash up before heading out to the bedroom. Patrick is still snuggled up in the bed, one arm thrown over his eyes to block the weak sunlight infiltrating our room. I pause, and take in the picture. It's rare that I get to see him sleeping because he's always up before me. He really is handsome—all muscles and lightly bronzed skin. His hair is mussed, making him look younger. The many facets of him boggle my mind, if I try to think about all the individual strands that make him up. Security Guard. Husband. Political Figure. False Identity. Killer. Lover. Protector. Peaceful, sleeping man. Somehow, they all tie together into this one, complicated, perfect package.

Patrick stirs, and his eyes blink open, taking me in as I loiter in the bathroom doorway. "Morning," he says, voice roughened from sleep.

"Good morning." I give him a small smile.

"Everything okay? You're not usually up before me." He switches straight into overprotective mode, one of the things I've come to love about him.

I never have to wonder if he cares.

"Yep, just had to use the bathroom. Nothing to worry about." I slide back into the bed next to him, and sit against the headboard with my arms wrapped around my knees.

He studies my profile, an eyebrow raised. "Is it the pregnancy testing that's bothering you? Are you nervous that you could be pregnant already?" His voice is gentle, and he rubs a soothing hand along my thigh.

"No, it's not that, actually. To be honest, I haven't really thought about it too much. It's so soon, it's unlikely to happen yet, right?" I pause, thinking it over. "I mean, I know it happened for Teddy and Faith, but, deep down I don't feel like it will be that quick."

He gives my leg a gentle squeeze. "It will happen when it's meant to."

"Yeah, I think so, too." My voice is quieter now. "How much longer do you think it will take Glitch to figure out if he can hack into the security system? It's awful sitting around with this huge secret, and not being able to *do* anything. Josephine and Aisha, and all those other women—" The intense tightness in my throat cuts off the words abruptly.

Patrick scoots up to sit beside me, and wraps me in a hug. "I don't know, but hopefully not much longer," he says, and plants a kiss on the top of my head. "It is awful to wait, but there's not much else we can do for now. I've been racking my brain trying to come up with a way to get us safely out of here and figure out where we'd even go. And my dad—what do I tell him? *Should* I tell him?" His arm tightens reflexively.

I can tell how much he hates the idea of his dad having any part of this evil, but as the prime minister, we can't rule out his involvement. "I know, Patrick. *Somebody* authorized this, though, and unfortunately until we figure out who, we can't risk it." I hesitate, hating to be a hypocrite, but needing to say the thing nagging at my brain. *I still want to tell Peter.*

He sighs. "I know, you're right, but I can't believe he would have anything to do with this. My dad wouldn't hurt a fly." He runs a frustrated hand through his hair, and a section is now sticking straight up.

With a giggle, I zhuzh it until it lays back down. His crooked grin in response is enough to make my heart melt into a puddle. Guilt stabs at me instantly—it's not right to be happy, when we know what we do.

He must sense my quicksilver mood change, because he nudges me with his shoulder. "What's wrong, Sadie? You never did say."

"It's Aisha."

"You mentioned her name before, but I don't know her. Was she one of the women we found?"

I nod and rest my chin on my knees.

"Was there something in particular about her that's bothering you?" he asks.

"I forgot to tell you, right after. But, I knew her. From home." The words don't want to come out, but the fear and pain don't want to stay bottled up inside anymore.

"I didn't realize. That must make this even harder for you—the waiting." He brushes a wisp of my hair back from my face so he can see me better.

I nod, the sharp stab in my chest agreeing with him. "She didn't want to go. She waited, like me. Came at the last minute, and they told her parents she was dead. Died delivering a baby boy, and that they couldn't adopt him. They gave the baby away to a couple in the adoption program, and her parents got . . . nothing. Not her, not the baby, nothing but a letter full of lies."

He makes an angry sound, low in his throat.

"It could just as easily have been me, Patrick. Lying in that bed, pregnant against my will, and drugged up. She came from my town, rode the same *shuttle*, for Pete's sake. She probably even met Todd." I sit up now, my anger taking over the fear that threatens to consume me. "She's been gone for *years*. Years of her life eaten up, and she doesn't even know. Even if we somehow figure out a way to stop this, Patrick, that's irrevocable. We can't give her those years back. And, Lord have mercy, the *babies*." The emotions finally win, and tears begin to trail down my cheeks. I choke on a sob, my futile attempt to hold it in failing.

Patrick pulls me into his chest and rests his chin atop my head. He holds me tightly, but doesn't say anything.

"She's had four babies, Patrick. Four. She has four children out there being raised by unknowing strangers. They don't even know she's alive. If we expose this, free these women, waking them up isn't going to be a kindness. We're going to wake them up, and have to tell them something that's going to destroy them." The last bit is hardly above a whisper. The reality is so ugly, so cruel, I can barely voice it into this world.

I sob into his chest, my heart shattered to pieces for all of the innocent lives that have been irreversibly altered by this horrendous place. He holds me until I've cried myself out, not complaining about the mess I've made of his t-shirt, or the fact that I didn't even let him out of bed yet. His slow, soothing strokes of my hair eventually ground me, bringing me back to the present moment. I slowly sit up, and wipe the tears from my cheeks.

When I lock eyes with him, his expression is so cold, it's almost scary. "What is it, Patrick? What are you thinking?"

"Someone is going to be held accountable for what's been done to them, Sadie. I swear it. I will do everything in my power to make this right. We can't give them back the years they lost, no. But we can find their children, we can wake them up, and we can help them start over. We can tear this place apart, and make sure it *never* happens again." His voice is fierce, and the menacing intent gives me goosebumps as he cups my cheek in his hand.

"Thank you, Patrick. Thank you for helping make this right." Tears well up again, but this time, it's gratitude. Gratitude that even though I never intended to have a match like Patrick, he's the right man to tackle this problem with me.

"Don't thank me, Sadie. It's the right thing to do—what anyone *should* do." His jaw is set in grim determination, and I can tell he's questioning his father's involvement again.

It's my turn to reassure him, so I lay a hand on his shoulder. The tension I feel could snap a branch. "Patrick, I am sure when we find out who is doing this, it's not going to be your dad. We will figure it out as soon as we can, and then we'll let him help us fix this. Surely he's in a position to help make this right, as quickly as possible."

His shoulders sag almost imperceptibly under my touch. "I hope you're right."

"I'm right. Now, what do you say we go get some breakfast? I'm starving. Also, we have a urine sample to deliver." I roll my eyes, which draws a chuckle out of him.

Breakfast, as always, is delicious. The wait staff have become accustomed to our preferences now, so most things, we don't even have to ask for. Peter joins us, and Martinez hovers in the doorway, looking bored. I've just leaned back from the table, rubbing my very full stomach when Peter changes the subject abruptly.

"So, are you two ready for your outing today?" he asks, and wags his eyebrows at us.

"What outing? It's not more hiking, is it?" I look at Patrick, feeling cold even thinking about hiking in this weather. It's gray and gloomy outside, with whipping wind.

"Peter, my man, you're killing my surprise here," Patrick complains, but doesn't sound angry. He shoots an exaggerated cut-it-out look at Peter before addressing me. "Sadie, I scheduled something new to get your mind off of things. We've got a shuttle to catch, as soon as we're done with breakfast."

I lean forward, interest piqued. "What kind of outing are we talking about? You have to tell me, I hate surprises!"

He shakes his head stubbornly. "No way, no how. You'll have to wait and see."

"Oh, come *on*! Peter knows! How is that fair?"

His grin is devious. "Peter has to know, to make sure it's safe before we leave the property. You'll find out when we get there."

"Ugh, fine. Well, let's go now, then. I'm done. You're done, too." I gesture at his empty plate.

"Not yet, I still have half my coffee left!" He gestures to one of the staff for a refill, but I wave them away before they take two steps in our direction.

"No way! You torture me with a surprise, you don't get extra coffee. Peter, you should go call Todd. We're ready."

Peter laughs, but doesn't budge. "Ahh, baby sister. Torturing you never gets old." His grin is the biggest I've seen it since the first day he got here.

"Peter, you cannot be on his side. You're my brother, for Pete's sake. Come on! Where is your family loyalty?" I cross my arms over my chest.

He shrugs noncommittally. "Patrick's a good guy. He's grown on me."

"Well, if you're not on my side anymore, I guess next time I see Mom I'll have to tell her about the time that Nancy Locken *grew on you* your senior year. I feel like that story still has the shock factor, no matter when it comes out."

He stills, jaw dropping. "You wouldn't. I swore you to secrecy! Plus, I had no control over that. She was nuts! How was I supposed to know she'd climb through *your* bedroom window looking for me on Christmas Eve?"

Patrick barks out a surprised laugh. "Who's Nancy Locken?"

"I was so excited, thinking it was Santa coming in with presents. But was it Santa Claus? No. It was Nancy Locken wearing a Santa Claus *costume.*"

Peter drops his head into his hands. "Please don't tell Mom this story. I'm pretty sure she'll retroactively kill me."

Feeling my imminent win, I continued. "She was obsessed with Peter, and he let her think he might consider going out with her in the New Year after break. She couldn't wait and decided to try to speed things along. She not only scared the living daylights out of me, but she ruined Santa. I was *eight.*"

"We're going to do a tour of the farm down the road that supplies all the produce here." Peter's voice comes out muffled through his hands, but the victory is sweet regardless.

Patrick looks between us incredulously. "Just like that, seriously Peter? One little story and she gets whatever she wants?"

I pump my fists in the air with excitement. "Yes! Farm tour! Let's go already!" I grab Patrick by the arm, and he reluctantly puts down his mug and follows me.

Peter pushes back his chair with a scrape and stands to follow us. "Sorry, man, my mom can never know about Nancy. That story is going with me to my grave."

I'm still grinning ear to ear as we board the shuttle a minute later, and Todd greets us politely. Patrick's look is speculative as we choose the loveseat in the middle of the shuttle. "You have a devious side to you, Sadie Royce."

"Dang straight. And don't you forget it."

We drive for nearly an hour, and the surroundings get shabbier the further we are from the resort. Immediately outside, everything was nicely manicured and kept up. After about ten minutes, you could tell the closers had done their jobs, and everything looked frozen in time, like an unruffled snow globe. But this far out, the area is starting to go back to the wild. The last few houses we've passed have trees sprouting through them, collapsed roofs, and were so wildly grown up in some cases you could hardly tell there had been a home before. It's both sad and impressive, to see nature taking back over what humanity once thought they owned. Turns out, we are nothing more than a blip on the earth's timeline. Flaring brightly for a time, but now blinking out.

Then, out of the wildness the familiar sight of tended pastures comes into view. The road winds, and a wooden archway announces we've arrived at Branch Farms. The shuttle slowly bumps onto the narrow drive, and we meander back to a faded red farmhouse with clapboard siding. The pastures lining each side of the drive are dotted with various farm animals, all spread out and enjoying the sunshine. My heart warms at the sight, and the homesickness that wells up inside of me can't be denied.

I look over at Patrick and find him perusing me instead of the surroundings. "Thank you for setting this up. It's lovely here."

He smiles, and the genuine warmth he has for me edges out the homesickness bit by bit. Perhaps home really is where the heart is, because there's no denying that a piece of my heart has been claimed by the man in front of me. "I hoped it would make you happy, to get away from the resort for a while." He leans in and kisses me on the forehead. "Come on, let's go explore."

I happily hop from my seat, and nudge a snoring Peter with my foot before walking to the front. "Some ferocious guard you are, sleeping on the job."

He jolts to attention, and takes in our new location. "Hey, I had the late shift last night. And moving vehicles are my Achilles' heel. Martinez was on duty for the drive." He rubs his eyes with the heel of his hand before standing and stretching. "I'm ready to go. What are we even doing at this place? It just looks like a farm, no different than back home."

I sigh with contentment. "Exactly."

I exit the bus with a pep in my step, and suck in a lungful of the sweet, grassy air. The pungent scent of farm animals mingles with it, and while many wouldn't find that pleasant, for me it's like coming home. I look around, greedily taking in the sights of this beautiful farming setup. They've got large pastures cross-fenced along the entire front, but behind the house I see several of the most enormous geometric greenhouses I've ever seen. They are all reflecting light, and at stark odds with the well-worn home they sit behind.

As I'm staring in awe at the behemoth glass structures, a woman with a graying bun atop her head and well-worn flannel shirt comes out of the house with the slap of the screen door. "Hey, y'all. You must be from the honeymoon resort," she says in a friendly tone. "I'm Marie Branch, owner of the farm here and your tour guide today." She walks right up and shakes hands with each of us in turn. Her grip is firm, and her hands are calloused. "My husband and son are around here somewhere, so I'll introduce them when we run into them."

"Hi Marie, nice to meet you! I'm Sadie, and this is Patrick, Peter, and Martinez. Hey, what's your first name, actually?" It hits me that I don't know it, but definitely should.

He snorts. "You can call me Martinez."

"Okay, then, Martinez it is. Now, have any of you ever been to a farm before? Because we have some ground rules," Marie says.

"Yes! Our family owns and runs a ranch out of Jackson Flats! I'm so excited to see your setup and what you do differently up here that we might be able to try out at home. Well, when we eventually make it home, anyways." My happy chatter trails off with the reality rushing in that this is going to be a great day, but it's still only one day.

This isn't forever. Try to enjoy it while it lasts. I shake off my wave of gloom. Patrick worked his magic to make this day happen for me, and I'm going to enjoy every minute.

"Well, that's fantastic! I wondered why we suddenly got a tour request, but that makes much more sense. We've been supplying the resort since they opened it, and never once had a couple come out to visit. We're mighty glad to have you. Since you know what you're doing, I'll skip the boring stuff. So, if you run cattle at home, would you rather start off with the mobile milk shed or the hydroponic farm?"

I look over at Patrick with unfettered glee. "Hydroponics! Is that what's in those massive shiny greenhouses?"

She chuckles at my childlike enthusiasm. "Sure is. Come on, we'll start over there."

Our farm tour speeds by in a blur of sunshine, grass, and cutting-edge farm technology. The amount of knowledge Marie has about sustainability and food culture and preservation is mind-boggling, even to a rancher like me. We have to worry about herd genetics and diversity, but she's got to keep hundreds of different plant species thriving, seeds to collect and store, and pollination rates to calculate that leave me reeling. It is hands down my favorite activity, outside of riding Hercules, that we've done in all the months of being away from home.

Then, as the icing on the cake, she served us an absolute feast for lunch with fresh-made bread, wild berry jam, and a pecan pie to finish everything off. I am stuffed to the gills, and enjoying my back porch rocking chair while I digest. Martinez wandered off to give Drake and Don a hand with some heavy lifting, and Marie told us to sit a spell while she catches up on office work, so it's just the three of us on the back porch for the moment.

I take in the rolling pastures and clucking chickens and realize that this is the most alone we've been with Peter since he's arrived. Living in the guest house is safer, but gives no privacy away from the ever-present staff and personal guard detail.

"Peter, we need to talk to you about something." Patrick's head snaps up, but Peter keeps watching the chickens squawk and tussle over the crust bits he's tossing into the yard.

"Lay it on me, baby sister. Wait, no mushy stuff, right?" He cringes and then keeps tossing bread.

"No, it's serious, though." Patrick grimaces, but nods for me to continue.

My tone must convey the import, because he tosses the last hunk of bread and wipes his hands before turning his chair to face mine. "Okay, what's up?"

I start at the beginning, with Josephine getting hauled out of the announcement back at the NLC. By the time I get to the part about finding the medical facility in the forest, his face is blanched white, and his hands are clasped so tightly in front of him I think he might break something.

"Sweet Jesus in heaven" is all he says for a long moment after I finish the story. He looks to Patrick, whose grim expression matches mine. "How are they getting away with it? How can they . . ." He trails off and rubs one hand over his face wearily. "You said there's more? More women, more facilities?"

Patrick is first to respond. "Yes, Glitch has a list of names and locations all over the continent. He's trying to get in and get footage of what's going on, but he hasn't had any luck yet."

"What are you planning to do with the footage? We can't let this keep happening." His expression turns thunderous. "Lord, poor Aisha's been gone for years, hasn't she? Her parents had a funeral, what, three years ago now? I was home on leave at the time, and I still remember thinking that they looked like ghosts."

I nod, remembering the awful day well.

"We don't have a solid plan yet, but we all agree we can't stop this from inside the resort. I'm pretty sure our movements and conversations are being monitored. We have to get solid proof so no one can cover this up, and then figure out the best way to stop this without hurting anyone. We've got to get those women out, not get them killed in a cover up."

"I know it seems logical, but that is going to be hard to pull off, given that I'm supposed to be guarding you with my team twenty-four-seven to keep the crazies at bay." His voice is agitated as he continues, "To top it off, this cannot look like an escape attempt, or you could end up in a detention facility—or worse, one of these secret facilities—if you're caught."

"Well, we've got to figure something out. It makes my skin crawl every time I walk in the door of the guest house and everyone's just hovering and smiling at us. Because I know it's fake now. There are women exactly like me, who walked the same halls, drugged less than a mile away." I rub my arms, the sudden chill making my skin pebble uncomfortably.

Peter rubs his face wearily again, but even having that much appalling information dropped into his lap, he doesn't lose his composure. Instead, he snaps into action mode. He leans forward intently, forearms on knees, and his words fly out in a low staccato barrage.

"Okay, you're going to have to leave. Fine. We can figure out an escape plan. But how do we ensure the safety of the group, and where are you going to go? There are only a few places in the NAA that might be a possibility. But now that you've done that interview and the whole country has seen the two of you . . . that poses a problem."

I blow out a frustrated breath at the reminder of Candy's unpleasant interrogation. Excuse me, *interview*.

Patrick breezes past that into the details. "I think Calivada. It's the only central place where there's already enough unrest to have loosened the NAA police's hold."

"Wait, what? What do you mean there's unrest in Calivada? I haven't seen anything about it on the news."

Peter snorts. "Sadie, do you really think that NAA One would be allowed to report that? When things don't go well for the politicians, they don't exactly like that to be wide-spread knowledge." He darts a glance at Patrick. "No offense. It's just the facts."

He waves off the slight. "None taken, I have no desire to be a politician. Ever since things started to collapse, non-essential jobs have declined rapidly to keep people trained as doctors and scientists and food producers. It made sense to only have one news outlet, but I won't pretend that hasn't been exploited over the last century."

I probably shouldn't be shocked at this revelation, but it never occurred to me that the media might be hiding things from us. It's literally their job to inform us of things. *If the news is run by politicians, how are we going to broadcast footage of the imprisoned women even if we get it?*

"Back to Calivada—I think it's a good choice. You might have to work on a disguise of some kind, but there are definitely fewer people there willing to call in the police to out you. Nobody wants us around out there," Peter says, steepling his fingers together.

"Atlas is making some calls to some contacts he has out there, to see how we might best get out of here, and be hidden in plain sight. He's done some jobs for some very influential people, and he thinks he might be able to get us a house to hole up in, at least until we make a more concrete plan."

Peter nods. "It's a good start. I can work with him on an exit strategy. How close is Glitch to getting that footage, do you think? This isn't the kind of thing it's good to sit on for long. Somebody *always* finds out."

Patrick's grimace says it all. "I've got bad news on that front. He's hit some kind of block with trying to tap into the security network. He doesn't think it's insurmountable, but it's not going to be fast. The last time we spoke he said something about a great wall of illusion and chicanery. I have no idea what that meant, but it didn't sound good."

"That's not the end of the world. If he is trying to hack remotely now, he can keep digging once you're all safely out from under the constant observation, and risk of being snatched yourselves. Until we can get you out, you'll have to stay under the radar and keep following orders. Actually—"

Peter's face is serious, but his next thought is cut off by a creaking screen door. "All right love birds—and love birds' brother—who's ready to finish up our tour?"

I paste on a smile and quickly rise from my rocking chair, but the formerly delightful tour now feels a bit hollow. "I'd love to! What's next?"

She loops her arm through mine, and we stroll down the back porch steps together. "Well, considering that you're on your honeymoon and working on starting a family of your own, I thought I'd save the best for last. Would you like to see the baby barn?" she asks with a lopsided smile.

The guys trail right behind us, and Patrick asks, "What's a baby barn?"

"It's where we keep all the little ones who aren't big enough to be with the herds or flocks yet, or out in the cold weather. We don't have many this time of year, but we've got a fresh hatch of chicks and a few goats that came out of season."

"I would love to see the baby barn!" I gush, hoping it doesn't sound too forced. *Try to enjoy the rest of the day, Sadie. There won't be many like this for a while.* I remind myself, but it's hard to flip the switch like that.

Marie leads us to a small, freshly-painted red barn. It looks like someone plucked it right out of a children's picture book, with a hay-loft window above the white double doors. As soon as she pulls the door open, a flurry of chirps flood my ears. As my eyes adjust to the dimmer interior lighting, I catch my first glimpse of the yellow and black fuzzy masses of chicks in an enclosure right inside the door.

"Oh my word, there are so many!" My excitement is real this time, because the cuteness can't be denied.

"Yeah, we always hatch as large a batch as we can in the winter, so they have plenty of buddies to keep them warm." She gestures to the red heat lamps spaced around the room, when a hard thump lands on the back of my knee.

Turning in surprise, I see that my assailant is a tiny, spotted goat. He bleats, and walks his front legs up mine to sniff my hands. I squat down to give him a scratch, and he bleats again.

Marie shakes her head at the demanding fellow. "That's Milo. He's a ham." She comes over and tosses a few handfuls of millet to the chicks, and then gives me a small biscuit for Milo.

He munches it greedily, before butting me again. "Aren't they cute, Patrick?" I look around for my unusually silent husband, and find him with both hands in his pockets, standing uncomfortably behind me. Marie scoops up a chick and offers it to him.

"Oh, no, thank you. I'll just watch. I don't know anything about babies, or baby animals." His discomfort surprises me.

"It's all right, Patrick. They're not going to bite you," I say, accepting the little cheeping fluff ball from Marie. "Besides, what are you going to do when we have a baby? Never hold it?"

His eyebrows shoot up his forehead in a comical expression. "Uh, well . . . is that an option?"

Marie full-out belly laughs. "No, hon, it's not." She claps him on the shoulder with a grin. "And you'll be even more terrified to hurt your baby than you are these. So, buck up and hold out your hands."

He reluctantly cups his hands, and she deposits a fuzzy black chick in them. His eyes widen, but otherwise he stays stock still.

"Don't let him jump, he'll break a leg from that height," she says matter-of-factly.

He quickly cups his hands more deeply so the chick can't escape. It peeps in protest but doesn't make a run for it. Shaking my head at the amusing sight, I look around for Peter. I find him, squatted down and mobbed by three baby goats. He is handing out cookies and pats as fast as he can. One of them buts the back of his arm, and he chuckles and gives it the next cookie.

As suspected, you can take the man away from the country to police training, but you can't train the country out of him.

We play with the babies until Martinez, Drake, and Don come and tell us they've finished with the new automatic waterer they were working on out in the pasture.

Martinez has sweated through his uniform, so I'm sure he'll enjoy the hour-long drive home. He doesn't look unhappy, though. Much to my surprise, Patrick is reluctant to hand off the little black chick when it's time to leave. Marie gives him a warm smile. "He's really grown on you, huh? Why don't you name him?"

"It's a him?" he asks, giving the tiny bird a stroke on his soft head.

"Yep, they aren't usually this fat unless they're males."

He thinks about it for a minute. "How about Pepper?"

"Pepper's perfect." She smiles before gently putting Pepper back in with his abundant siblings.

It's with genuine sadness, and a whole pie, that we board the shuttle back to the resort. I give Marie a hug, her embrace reminding me of my last hug with mom, the few months away feeling like an eternity.

"Y'all are welcome back any time. But next time, we'll put you to work." She shakes a finger at us with mock sternness.

"I would love that! I need to see that hydroponics setup again, and my parents would be thrilled if I learned enough to set something similar up back home. We don't have much going on in the way of fish in our area, so that would be huge for us."

"Well, it's a date then." She lays my collar flat and pats me on the shoulder in a mothering gesture which causes my heart to squeeze again. "If there are more girls like you in this program, maybe it won't be so bad for Drake after all." Her eyes are sad at the thought.

I take her hands in mine. "I have met some lovely women in this program. There are a few bad apples in any bunch, but for the most part, we all want a family, and a normal life."

She looks relieved at that.

We all settle back into the bus's love seats, except Martinez who goes to change in the back. Todd whistles a peppy tune as we bump back down the driveway, and I stare longingly at the lovely pastures slipping away from us.

"Don't worry, Sadie, we'll come back. Maybe we can convince the director to let us stay a few days. Drake mentioned that they have a guest house," Patrick says, rubbing my shoulders in a comforting gesture.

The idea sounds lovely, but even this home-away-from-home is a placeholder for what I really want. *Soon, hopefully. It's not forever.*

Patrick's pocket buzzes, and he withdraws his mini-tablet. I'd left mine in our room. "Your presence is requested in the guest house at your earliest convenience," he reads off. "Huh, wonder what that's about?" he says, tipping it towards me so I can see the swirling script.

"No clue. Maybe we can squeeze in a nap before we get back and find out." I lean my head on his shoulder, and stare out the window at the wild tree line sliding past. The ruins of an overgrown house are the last thing I see as my eyes close, the sound of Peter's rhythmic snores from a few rows up lulling me to sleep as well.

EIGHTEEN

HIT THE FAN

T he loud squealing of tires wakes me from my sleep, coupled with the terrifying feeling of falling and hurtling forward. I jolt and reach out with my arms to stop my descent. A long moment passes as I try to work out our location. The last thing I remember is falling asleep, watching the sunset out the window over the ruins of old houses sliding by. In the chaotic moment I awaken, not much time seems to have passed based on the still-growing dark. However, the sounds and sights surrounding me are starkly different.

In addition to the grating screech of the shuttle's tires on pavement, Peter's shouts echo in my ringing ears, over what sounds like helicopter blades ahead of us on the road. Time seems to slow as the bus shimmies side to side, and in a detached way I notice that for the first time ever, Todd does not seem happy as he stands with both feet on the brake pedal, trying to stop the shuttle. My eyes dart to the front windshield and see a bevy of black vehicles blocking the road—and Todd is trying to avoid a collision. He tries to turn, but a few shoot past us before we've even cleared the blacktop, driving down the shoulder toward the rear of the shuttle, and he has to stop to avoid smacking one. The chopper sound is growing steadily louder, so I try to look out the window to see what's up there. Patrick grabs me and snatches me back from the glass.

"Stay down, Sadie. We don't know who's out there." The shuttle shakes as it comes to a final stop, and Patrick shoves me to the floorboards, crouching over the top of me. Patrick and Peter are yelling something, but the ringing in my ears still has not subsided enough for me to comprehend what about. Are we being kidnapped? Is this another attempt by the people who bombed the resort? Peter's voice finally breaks through the buzzing and I hear him barking commands at Martinez through his wrist comm.

"We've got at least six hostiles, I repeat, six hostiles on ground crew and they've got aerial backup. I repeat, they have wings. I need a full guard rolling out stat. The crown jewels are in imminent danger!" Peter's voice is strained as the shuttle bus rocks from side to side and a boom sounds.

"Sadie, do not move from this spot, do you understand me?" Patrick's voice is low and deadly calm.

"Yes, I won't move." I try to keep my voice steady, but I fail miserably. He squeezes my shoulder, and darts across the aisle while crouching low to avoid being a target through the windows. I curl into the fetal position on the ground, and watch as Peter hands him a pistol from under the loveseat, and Patrick is back hovering over me a moment later.

"It's going to be okay, Sadie, we have to hold tight until backup gets here from the resort." The shuttle rocks again, and the boom is louder this time. "They want us alive—they aren't going to try to kill us. We just have to hang in there." He rests his palm in the middle of my back, steadying me when it feels like the whole shuttle might tip over from the repercussion.

"Are you sure about that? It seems to me like they're trying to blow us up!" I shout over the racket.

"Yes, I'm sure. The grenades are stopping short. They're trying to flush us out so they can grab us. They don't know how many of us are armed. It's actually a good thing that they're not rushing in here, it gives our backup time to get here."

Peter has edged up to the window and is peering out to take measure of our enemies. He swears under his breath, and that's when I know we're in deep trouble. Peter never swears.

"Patrick, take Sadie down the aisle and to the emergency exit by the left rear bathroom. On my signal, you pop the hatch and you head to the woods. Take shelter, and don't come out no matter what you hear."

"Peter, I am not going anywhere without you." I can hear the shrillness rising in my own voice as panic claws at my throat.

"Patrick, do you understand? You are not to leave whatever shelter you find and you are not to let her out of arm's length at any time, copy?" Peter ignores my objection, and I feel like I can't breathe at the insinuation.

Patrick's response is low and hard. "Copy."

Peter ignores us now. "Martinez, I count 12 head up front, plus aerial support. What's your rear count?"

There is a short pause and then Martinez shouts from the rear, "Seven rear."

"Peter, we're not going to make it past that many people by ourselves. We're not leaving you, Peter. I won't do it."

Patrick grips me by the upper arms and hauls me to a sitting position. "Sadie, you don't argue with the commanding officer in combat."

"He is not my commanding officer, he is my brother and I WILL NOT LEAVE HIM!" I scream right in his face, but he never gets a chance to respond, because Peter's shout cuts him off.

"TAKE COVER!"

Patrick throws himself on top of me, and rolls us against the foot of a love seat right before the loudest explosion yet causes the entire shuttle to lurch up and over onto its side in a massive jolting impact. The motion tosses us all like rag dolls through the shuttle and we slam into the windows, now flush against the grassy shoulder of the road. Shattered glass lands in my hair, and a hissing sound of some sort is the first thing to register after the impact.

I landed on top of Patrick, so I push up on my elbows and try to climb off of him quickly, but my limbs are leaden. Finally I get off of him, and he lurches to a sitting position.

"Sadie, are you okay?" I can barely hear him, but I nod. He has a gash on his cheek that is bleeding steadily, but otherwise he looks okay.

Peter's voice reaches us from the front of the shuttle. "Todd is out. Everyone else report!"

"We're bruised but in one piece." Patrick answers for us, and from the back of the shuttle, silence is Martinez's only answer.

Oh God, they don't care if they take us alive. We're not getting out of this.

Glass crunches under Peter's black boots as he hauls an unconscious Todd on his shoulders to where we're crouched mid-shuttle. He lays him at our feet, oblivious to the crushed glass. "Stay here, I'll get Martinez." He bounds to the back of the shuttle and hauls himself up the bathroom wall and settles in a crouch before dropping into the bathroom out of sight.

My gaze lands on the unconscious Todd, and I'm relieved to see that he's breathing. Blood is coming out of a cut on his temple, and the ear underneath. I'm not a doctor, but that can't be a good thing. Patrick, still in a crouch, has crossed the shattered windows to the roof emergency hatch to test the handle.

His first effort doesn't work, but with a grunt he manages to wrench it open. My relief at the apparent exit is snatched away by the smell of burnt rubber and acrid black smoke that pours into the open hatch.

"Peter, you've got to get out here! Something's on fire!" I shout. His head and shoulders appear out of the door frame, and he quickly scrambles out. Martinez doesn't follow. "Where's Martinez?" I ask, watching over his shoulder, but the other man doesn't emerge.

His only response is a sharp shake of the head.

Lord help us all. He died to protect us, and Todd's unconscious.

"What's on fire?" He's all business, despite his fallen comrade.

"The shuttle. We're going to have to run for it." Patrick's expression is grim.

"Okay, you've got Sadie, I've got Todd. The good news is the explosion put us closer to the tree line. The bad news is, they've had time to move closer while we've been regrouping. It's now or never." He turns to me, and snatches me into an unyielding hug. "I love you, baby sister. Don't ever forget it." He releases me and in one motion shoves me backwards into Patrick's waiting arms. He then moves to the hatch, and peers around the corner cautiously.

"Okay, I'm going to lay down cover fire. When you clear the tree line, you can return the favor and then you run like a tsunami is coming after you. You hear me? You do not stop. You do not turn around, and you do not, for any reason, look back. Sadie, I mean it. Do. Not. Stop. Running."

"Peter, you have to come with us." His mouth is set in a line, and he doesn't respond, just gets into position with his gun. The black metal gleams in the flickering light of the growing fire at the front of the shuttle. The smoke has grown thicker inside, and my lungs burn in disapproval.

"Peter, I mean it, I won't go without you!"

Patrick hauls me into position, so we've got a clear shot at the opening when Peter signals.

"Peter, I'm serious. Peter, look at me!"

He spares a quick glance at me, before training his eyes back on whatever he's watching outside. "Sadie, I'll be right behind you. My job is to guard you, and I intend to do just that. But you have to run as fast as you can, or they'll catch us all."

I let out a relieved breath. All in one motion, Peter shoves the hatch as wide as it will go and starts spraying bullets in a wide arc at targets we can't see. "Move! Move! Move!"

Patrick's grip on my hand might have bruised it if I wasn't gripping his just as hard in return when we bolt out the hatch at a full sprint. My heart pounds, and the tree line still seems too far away for us to make it with all of the gunfire piercing the night around us. I trip over a hole in the ground, twisting my ankle in the process. Patrick barely slows, just enough to keep me on my feet and keeps his eyes trained forward. We're barely ten yards from the trees when a black aircraft appears above us, the sound of chopping blades our only warning before dust and dirt fly into our eyes from the wind.

It's not a helicopter as I'd originally thought, but some sort of large cargo airship. The gunfire ceases, or I can't hear it any more, as the deafening sound of the airship hovers directly above us. My lungs burn as we push even harder, but the buffeting wind slows us. A spotlight floods us with blinding light, and my steps falter again as the ground in front of us seems to wash out in an instant. My free hand flies to my eyes, trying to gain visibility, but it's futile.

Before I even realize what's happening, a sound like 12 giant zippers being undone at once surrounds us, and a platoon of black-masked men land on all sides.

"Sadie, look out!" I hear Peter's hoarse scream and look back to see him directly outside the circle of assailants, Todd nowhere to be found.

He's grappling with two of them and holding his own, and I turn to run back to him when Patrick's hand is wrenched painfully from mine. The force spins me around, and arms like steel bands wrap around me from behind. "No, no!" I scream, as I look down and see that it's not Patrick who has me, but one of the attackers. I kick and thrash with all my might, but the man's grip is like iron, and he doesn't flinch when my boots connect with his shins.

My frantic eyes land on Patrick, with two men holding his arms, while a third snatches a bag over his head. "Patrick!" The useless scream is torn from my lips, and I see him jerk in response. One of the arms caging me comes up to slap a hand over my mouth.

Realizing this might be my only chance, I bite down on his hand until the coppery tang of blood hits my tongue, and the hand is snatched away. With all my might, I kick backwards towards the man's groin, and his arm drops away. I sprint towards Patrick, my only thought to free him so we can get out of here. Aiming for the closest man, I throw all of my weight at him right where he's clutching Patrick's arm. Surprise works in our favor, because he's knocked clear of Patrick and we land in a tangle on the ground. I try to roll away, but he grabs my braid and snatches my head back. The searing pain in my scalp loses importance when he follows up with a meaty arm around my throat.

A bare trickle of air is making it to my starving lungs, and blackness starts to edge out the floodlights in my vision. Patrick once again has three men on him, and Peter is fighting three also, with one downed at his feet. He gets in a blow with the butt of his pistol and downs a second, but there are just too many. The men holding Patrick succeed in pinning his arms, and one of them uncaps a syringe with his teeth and plunges it deep into his neck. He stiffens with a jerk, and the last thing I see before blacking out is him crumpling backwards into his assailant's arms.

TAKING FLIGHT

I wake with a start, adrenalin still pumping from being captured by our kidnappers. My heart is beating wildly as I bolt upright, and am hit with a pounding headache right behind my eyes. Cradling my throbbing head with my hands, I scan my surroundings warily. I'm in a dark-paneled room with a closed door, sitting on a large bed which takes up almost all of the space, and to my utter shock Patrick is laid out next to me, unmoving. I crawl over to him with as much speed as my throbbing head will allow, and give him a gentle shake. He doesn't stir, so I feel for a pulse in his wrist. It's there, steady and even. A shaky breath escapes me, and I'm relieved that they've at least left us together and he seems to be stable, if still knocked out.

Another surprise, we're not restrained in any way. Although, we're probably locked in, so no need to restrain us. I scoot to the edge of the bed, and stand in the tight space between the bed and the wall. Gingerly making my way around—my whole body screaming from the abuse it's been through between the crash and abduction—I pause next to the door and listen, holding my breath. Muffled voices come through, and a low humming sound I can't place.

I reach over and gently twist the knob, which opens with a soft click. For a moment, I stare at it in shock. *What is going on here?* Steeling my nerves, I ease to the crack and peer out, expecting to see someone standing guard, but it's an empty hallway. Voices travel more clearly down it, now that I've cracked the door. I'm torn between exploring the area, or staying with Patrick. I straighten my shoulders, take a deep breath, and ease out into the hall. I pause for a moment, expecting an ambush that doesn't materialize.

The hallway is dark, with the dark metal walls gleaming in the faint light from the other end. Nylon netting hangs every few feet down the walls, and the floor is made of some sort of closely-packed grating. A few short inches below my feet, I can see pipes and wiring running in a tangle.

The voices are all localized to the other end of the short hallway, so I walk down it as quietly as I can. Light pours into the dim space from an open door. *They are making no attempt at subtlety, here. What is with these people?*

I flatten my back to the wall and breathe shallowly as I listen to an unfamiliar woman's voice, and one of the dangling nets tickles my cheek.

". . . your team operating with minimal casualties, given the odds stacked against this mission. It was tight, but we got there in time to pull it off. In the end, that's all that matters."

Anger rolls over me in a hot wave, but I force myself to focus. *You can be angry once you're safe.*

"Now, Mav tells me we're only about 20 minutes out, so we'll need to keep a tight perimeter at all times until our precious cargo is out of our hands. We're not out of the woods yet, and we need to stay sharp."

Twenty minutes out, from what? Are we still— My thought is cut off by a sudden dropping sensation of the ground beneath me, which causes me to stumble forward abruptly. I catch myself on the netting, but there's no doubt they heard me. Chairs scrape backwards, and I scramble back a few steps, but they're faster than I can move on my still-shaky knees. A black-clad woman with shining blonde hair appears in the doorway. Her garb is identical to our abductors; only her mask is missing.

"Sadie, fantastic. You should join us," she says, then spins on her heel and disappears back into the room.

I stand there, slack-jawed in my shock. That's it? You should join us? What in the ever loving heck is happening here?

"Sadie's awake?" I recognize the feminine voice that responds, but my brain is moving too slowly to piece this together.

I take a numb step forward, right as Nell comes barreling out of the room and nearly crashes into me.

"Sadie! Thank God you're awake. Are you okay? I mean, the doctor checked you and said you were okay, but, it's good to see for myself." She's rambling, and it's not helping my confusion or temper.

"Nell, what is going on? Did they kidnap you, too? And where are we?" I rub my still-pounding head—praying for relief and clarity—as she clasps my other hand in both of hers.

"Come on, Hel and Atlas will explain everything," she says confidently.

"Atlas is here, too?" I ask, following her into the bright room with a wince. The light feels like it pierces into my brain, and I barely stifle a groan.

The room has a conference table, surrounded by chairs, mostly filled with who I can only assume are our abductors. The blonde woman has taken a seat at the head of the table, and Atlas sits to her left. Nell leads me to his side.

"Atlas, what is going on? Do you know these people?"

He nods. "I do, but I didn't expect to see them so soon." His voice is even, unconcerned—and it's pissing me off.

"Care to explain why the heck these friends of yours ambushed us, and you're sitting here having a freaking cup of coffee with them?" I gesture accusingly at the steaming mug sitting in front of him.

"Allow me to introduce myself," the blonde woman purrs as she rises from her seat, interrupting us. "I'm Helena, but most everyone calls me Hel." She gestures at the men sitting around the table, several of them eyeing me warily.

"What do you want with us?" A small voice tells me I should back off, given they're probably all armed to the teeth. But anger has made me brash, and I find myself stepping forward until I'm toe to toe with Helena. Something about her rubs me the wrong way, and I am itching to blame what happened today on someone. *She'll do just fine.*

The mountainous man in the chair to her right rises, towering over us. She waves him off. "It's fine, Brock. She's understandably angry."

He settles back into his seat but doesn't take his eyes off of me.

"Since I can see you're not in a chatty mood, I'll cut right to the chase. Atlas reached out to us about scheduling an extraction and getting you four to a safe house." I dart a glance at Atlas, who nods once in confirmation. "We agreed it was best if this extraction happened in a way that would make the resort staff think one of the cult extremists had finally succeeded in grabbing you, valuable genetic prize that you are," she says drily. "So, when we heard rumors that another kidnapping attempt was going down today, well, we had to insert ourselves earlier than anticipated to snatch you before they did. They almost succeeded, too, blowing up the bus like that. They must be desperate to get you if they'd risk killing you to do it," she muses.

My mind is reeling. *If they aren't the extremist kidnappers, who the heck are they?*

"Anyway, we couldn't let them succeed, knowing that you have the information we need, never mind you being the only known Polymorph in existence."

I stiffen at her words. How does she know about my polymorphism? My accusatory glare lands on Atlas, but he gives me a minuscule shake of his head.

"Don't blame him. My people are well connected, and we found out through our own channels. We do our homework before stepping into something this big."

"Who are your people, exactly?" I ask, tired of beating around the bush and running on fumes. My adrenalin is finally wearing off, now that I know we're not in immediate danger.

"This, my girl, is the uprising. The only question now is if you're ready to rise with us."

To Be Continued

BEFORE YOU GO . . .

Thank you so much for reading Rise! Are you on the edge of your seat yet? The final book is out now, so you can get straight into it. I can't wait to hear what you think!

If you enjoyed this book, would you do me a HUGE favor, and leave a review? I know, I know —what to say? How to do it? I would really, truly appreciate it. I read every single review, and it means the world to me when readers take the time to leave a kind word, or some stars for a book. :)

If you'd like to keep in touch, you can find my newsletter here (https://www.subscribepage.com/e0v1b5), Facebook here(https://www.facebook.com/KAGandyAuthor), Instagram here(https://www.instagram.com/kagandyauthor/), and I'm also available by email at kagandyauthor@gmail.com.

MORE BY K. A. GANDY

Bea Mine (Sweet Nothings Bake Shop, Book 1)

Love Makes you Stupid. Bea's too smart to fall into Cupid's trap. Or is she?

Bea is in love with George Anderson. No two ways about it, she has been since she was seven years old, and first met her bestie's older brother. When the pair is thrust together for a long Valentine's Day of bakery deliveries, can they resist the spark—and frosting—that flies between them?

HEA Guaranteed! Clean, sweet, and wholesome reads.

Will Travel for Love (Sweet Nothings Bake Shop, Book 2)

Bea and George hit it off, but Daphne's still a party of one. Will she find her forever traveling companion, or be alone in paradise?

Check out book two of the Sweet Nothings Bake Shop series, and see what Celia's got up her sleeve for Daphne. Or should we say, who she's got up her sleeve?

Dwindle (Populations Crumble, Book 1)

Torn from her home and family. Forced to marry a genetically matched stranger. Will she find love, or destruction?

Rise (Populations Crumble, Book 2)

The man she thought she knew truly is a stranger. Swept away on their honeymoon, the stakes have never been higher. Will his identity be their undoing, or will they rise together?

Reign (Populations Crumble, Book 3)

Kidnapped from their honeymoon resort, nothing is as it seems. Betrayal, intrigue, and secrets abound as Sadie works to free the captive women. But will she end up the savior, or the next captive?

Sweet Romance Anthology (Paperback Only)

A heartwarming and swoon-worthy collection of 26 sweet, romantic short stories.

ABOUT THE AUTHOR

K. A. Gandy was born and raised in Jacksonville, Florida, and is married with two kids. She has worked as a restaurant hostess, library book shelver, ranch hand, tour guide, Realtor, tech whiz, landlord, and small business consultant, all in addition to pursuing her passion for writing. As a person of many interests, her life has never been boring. She likes to write late in the evenings and thinks drinking hot tea and baking great cookies fuels hopes and dreams. If you would like to find more of her works, you can sign up for her newsletter at https://www.subscribepage.com/e0v1b5. You can also get updates on Facebook at https://www.facebook.com/KAGandyAuthor.

www.ingramcontent.com/pod-product-compliance
Lightning Source LLC
Chambersburg PA
CBHW022007050726
47499CB00003BA/716